BENEVOLENT BREEZE

BY
ED ROBINSON

For the loyal readers of Breeze; your support has been invaluable, but this book is dedicated to **Leap of Faith**. We've been through a lot together. She's never let me down.

Benevolent;
Marked by or disposed to doing good.

Benevolence is the characteristic element of humanity.
Confucius

But friendship is precious, not only in the shade, but in the sunshine of life, and thanks to a benevolent arrangement, the better part of life is sunshine.
Thomas Jefferson

Every fresh act of benevolence is the herald of deeper satisfaction; every charitable act a stepping-stone toward heaven.
Henry Ward Beecher

One

A big motor yacht entered the bay at an unacceptable rate of speed. Its wake shook the anchored vessels violently. I watched in bemusement, wondering what kind of asshole was behind the wheel. I saw my fellow boaters struggle to hang on when it was their turn to suffer the huge waves the yacht was throwing off. "Hang on, Brody," I yelled. "Big wake coming."

The offending boat passed to our port by a hundred feet or less, heading for the flats. I didn't see anyone at the helm.

"Holy shit," screamed Brody. "What the hell!"

Three walls of water hit us broadside in succession. Dishes went flying and the salon table overturned. I grabbed the bridge ladder to keep from getting tossed overboard. I heard Brody go down, cussing. I peeked inside to make sure she was okay, before returning my stare to the culprit. The big yacht plowed into the shallow grass bed at speed and stuck fast. Its props continued spinning, digging up mud, and seagrass.

I helped Brody up and we hopped in the dinghy to go investigate. The boat's engines were still running as we approached. We tied off and climbed aboard. I found the captain on the floor of the upper helm. He was dead. Dead guys don't drive well. I didn't have to check for a pulse. Grey gore and blood was splattered everywhere. A handgun lay at the man's feet. Taped to the dash was a note. It was not a suicide note.

This vessel belongs to whoever finds it. There is signed paperwork below. Just sign your name to transfer the title.

There was no signature.

I shut down the engines and went below. Sure enough, I found a bill of sale and associated paperwork. I also found the owner's last will and testament. It was a hell of a way to start the day.

"You said you wanted a bigger, nicer boat," I said to Brody.

"Not like this," she said. "We better call the police."

One hour later, every law enforcement agency that had a boat was on the scene. We'd been careful to leave the scene untouched. The only prints we'd left were on the paperwork we'd found. I recognized one of the officers. He'd responded to this same grass flat when some boat thieves ran aground. As soon as I got the chance, I pulled him aside and showed him the note and the rest of it.

"We've got to stop meeting like this," he said.

"I sit here and mind my own business," I told him. "Shit just happens."

"Do you have the means to get this boat floating and out of here?" he asked.

"We can drag it off at the next big high tide," I said. "Don't you want to impound it or something?"

"Left to the county, it'll sit here and rot," he said. "We don't have a place to store it, and to be honest, I haven't the energy or the resources to get it off the mud."

"You could always call Sea Tow," I offered.

"So his wife and kids can fight over who gets the boat?" he said. "Just take the damn thing out of here. Make it simple for us. You've got the documents you need."

"Do you know who he is?" I asked.

"Prominent businessman," he said. "Up to his eyeballs in debt and corruption. It was all about to come down on him. Better this way I guess."

"No life insurance for suicides, though," I said. "What do you think there was to leave in his will?"

"Offshore accounts. Caribbean properties. Who knows?"

"Mind if I take a quick look?"

"I don't see how it would hurt anything," he said.

"Just curious," I said.

To my ungrateful daughter, Julia, I leave one United States dollar. Don't say I never gave you anything. To my long suffering wife, Jane, I leave the burden of winding down my financial matters. I'm sorry, the creditors will get most of it, but if there's anything left, it's all yours. I've enclosed account numbers for money you never knew about. I know I was a bastard, but now

I'm gone. Best wishes for a happy life without me. Jim Donaldson

"Guy sounds like a real prick," I said. "You'll make sure his wife gets this?"

"You take care of the boat," he said. "I'll take care of this."

That's how I became the not-so-proud owner of a fancy new yacht. It wasn't what I would have chosen, but it was worth an easy million. Brody wanted nothing to do with it, but she helped me clean up the mess and pull it into deeper water. The running gear appeared to be undamaged. I fired up the generator and turned on the air-conditioning. I pulled two Coronas out of the dead man's refrigerator and poked around inside. Jim Donaldson left very few clues as to who he was in life. The boat was luxurious, but with zero personal touches. It had a sterile feel to it, all stainless steel and leather. When Brody joined me I handed her a beer.

"What are we going to do with this thing?" she asked.

"We can always sell it," I said. "But I'd like to find a better purpose for it. Make some good come out of it."

"Donate it?" she asked.

"Maybe," I said. "But not to a charity. What do you think about finding just the right person to give it to? Someone who will really appreciate it."

"They'd have to be able to afford the upkeep and storage," she said. "Anyone down on their luck wouldn't have the money. No such thing as a free boat."

"Good point," I said. "But let's give it some more thought. There's got to be a way for someone to benefit from this."

"Still trying to balance the scales of justice?" she asked.

"I'm still deep in arrears in the karma department," I said. "Now the cosmic magician has dropped a million dollar yacht in my lap. He's trying to tell me to do something good with it."

I poked around until I found the ship's papers and a stack of owner's manuals for all the goodies onboard. The vessel was a 2008 Azimut 68S. She was powered by two huge V-12 MAN engines, each generating 1360 horsepower. The sales brochure claimed a cruising speed of thirty knots with a top speed of thirty-five knots. It had a single fuel tank that held eight hundred and forty-five gallons of diesel. The water tank had a capacity of two hundred and fifty gallons.

I took a tour below decks. I found the master stateroom midship. It featured a king-sized bed with a head and shower. A big LCD TV was mounted flush in the one wall. There was also a Bose Surround Sound system. A queen berth was forward with its own TV and sound system. The galley had every amenity that you'd find in a modern house. I noted the dishwasher and washer/dryer combo alongside the microwave, four-burner stove and full-size fridge.

Further down in the engine room I counted fourteen batteries. There was a panel that would allow the various systems to operate of both twelve and twenty-four-volt power. There was a big Kohler generator and a watermaker. It was equipped with a Halon fire suppression system. It had every conceivable extra goody a boat owner could ask for.

All the flooring, furniture and upholstery were first-class. It was a yachtie's yacht. It was mine, at least until the dead man's widow sent her lawyers looking for it. For the time being, it was in our possession. Hell, if I wanted to legally transfer ownership, I'd probably have to hire a lawyer myself. I didn't want that hassle, but I could put it to good use until the day of reckoning arrived.

What to do with it?

Brody went to work on the internet, searching ideas for a grand humanitarian mission. She'd picked up a new phone and assorted devices after our ordeal with the FBI ended. We'd both put a bullet into the hitman who was targeting us. Claiming that our victim was suspected of murders in various states, the FBI had quickly swooped in and claimed jurisdiction. It was quietly swept under the rug due to the fact that some rogue agent had hired him to kill us. Heads had rolled in Washington for other reasons since then. Director Wray remained and had knowledge of our circumstances. Brody was treated with kid gloves and assurances were made that we were safe to go on about our lives without fear.

The hitman was the second person I'd had a direct hand in killing. I felt no remorse over it, but taking a life is no small deed. "Thou Shalt Not Kill." I couldn't shake the feeling that I owed something to the mysterious forces of Karma. If I spent the rest of my life in charitable pursuit, would I ever even the scales? Could I do enough good to make up for my sins?

I pondered how the big yacht could help with my predicament. I wasn't sure yet what good a boat like that would be in my quest for redemption. Brody was thinking out loud as she scrolled through the internet.

"Lots of places in the Caribbean that still need help," she said. "Many communities are still rebuilding after Hurricane Irma."

"This is a big boat," I said. "But it's not equipped to haul lumber and construction supplies."

"Parts of Puerto Rico are still without electricity," she added.

"How can we help with that?" I asked.

"I don't know, just throwing things out there," she said.

"Keep thinking," I said. "Taking this yacht south to Puerto Rico doesn't sound too awful."

Later that day Brody presented me with a list. It was titled "Items Desperately Needed in Puerto Rico."

> Batteries, all sizes: (AAA, AA, D, C, etc.)
> Tarps, big enough to cover roofs
> Solar powered lights, fans, phone chargers
> Generators
> Diapers
> Feminine Hygiene Products
> Games and Toys for the children
> First Aid Kits

I looked around the interior of the Azimut. We could pack a ton of the items on the list. We could literally deliver a boatload of needed items. We could also do it quickly. We'd burn a bunch of fuel, but we could get there in a few days. We had the money to purchase as many items as we could fit aboard. We had the money for fuel.

"You want to do this?" I asked Brody.

"Let's do it," she said. "We need a place to park this beast where we can load her up."

"Our car is still at Palm Island Marina," I said. "But they've got no room for a boat this big."

"Does anyone around this area?"

"Not really," I said. "We can always anchor out, shuttle everything by dinghy."

"Sounds like a lot of unnecessary work," she said.

"Maybe we can rent a pontoon boat locally," I suggested. "That would cut down on the trips back and forth."

"Good idea," she said. "Now you're thinking. What's the draft on this thing?"

"The specs say five feet," I said. "We can anchor at Don Pedro, where we offloaded old Cecil's weed. You run back and forth to Walmart and I'll run back and forth to the boat on the pontoon. We'll have her loaded in a day or two."

"I'm excited," she said. "This will be fun."

"Barring bad luck or bad weather," I said.

"Shit works out, Breeze," she said. "Isn't that what you always say?"

"You're right," I admitted. "Let's get this thing ready to roll. I'll drive it and you can follow me with *Leap of Faith.*"

"Aye, aye, captain."

We sat together that evening to watch the sunset. I recalled all the times I sat there by myself, alone in the world. Things had changed since Brody and I threw in together. She was a true friend and partner. I'd never exactly had a surplus of friends. I supposed Holly was a friend. That was our problem. We'd been better friends than lovers. She was too much like a younger, female version of me. She was gone now, off to chase her own adventures and make her own memories.

The Three Amigos of Fort Myers Beach were friends of a sort. I came and went and we helped each other when the circumstances called for it. Captain Fred was the only one of the bunch that had done more for me than I'd done for him. We hadn't seen him or heard from him since our return from the Bahamas. He was likely too busy spending his money on the finer things in life.

Now Brody and I were set to traipse across an ocean to deliver aid to strangers in need.

Two

We soon realized that this venture would require some serious logistical planning. Loading up the yacht with supplies seemed an easy enough task, but distributing those supplies was another matter. We couldn't just walk through the countryside toting tarps and first aid kits. We needed to partner with aid organizations on the ground in order to benefit those most in need. This was clearly not my area of expertise. I left the research to Brody while I concentrated on the yacht's systems and capabilities. My talents were much more useful in that area.

My original idea was to blast across the Florida Straits north of Cuba and on to the Dominican. A simple straight shot over the open ocean was the shortest line between two points. Our new vessel had one significant handicap though. Its minimal fuel capacity and terrible fuel consumption rate made such a trip impossible. I dug around the helm looking for any records or a log that might be helpful. I found nothing. There was a fuel flow gauge in the dash. The only way to be certain of how much fuel she burned would be to take her out for a test run. We had just over a half a tank to play with.

We idled out the Boca Grande Pass, letting the big engines warm up. Once clear of the outside markers I opened them up. It took forever to level out on plane and the fuel burn was seventy gallons per hour. Once we evened out, I backed off the throttles, reducing our speed, and our fuel consumption. At a leisurely twenty knots per hour, she was burning fifty gallons of diesel per hour. It was the slowest speed we could maintain without falling off plane. We could run for sixteen hours at twenty knots, a total of 320 nautical miles. We'd have only forty-five gallons left in reserve at that point.

My grand plan to zip across the ocean was reduced to island hopping. Some of those islands would need to have fuel docks. The trip would take longer, and cost much more than anticipated. On a positive note, I was quite familiar with the island hopping route down through the Bahamas. Revisiting some of those places on a luxury yacht wouldn't be so bad.

I sat and studied charts that I'd examined many times before. I wanted to cut down on the number of short hops as much as possible in order to reduce the time involved to get to Puerto Rico. I came up with a possible shortcut. I carefully measured the distance from Marathon in the Florida Keys across the Cay Sal Bank, just below the southern tip of Andros, and on to George Town in the Exumas. It came out to just a tad over three hundred miles. Our reasonable effective range was three hundred and twenty. We'd be cutting it awfully close and leaving ourselves with precious little fuel in reserve. In calm weather, we could make it. If something went wrong we'd be in deep shit. I set about finding a way to store additional fuel, just in case.

Meanwhile, Brody had been on the phone with a dozen different agencies. Very few actually had people on the ground at this point. All admitted that many on the island still had no power and needed assistance. She switched her focus to local churches, but she encountered a language barrier outside of San Juan. The places needing help were mostly remote and far removed from the tourist attractions and beaches.

We took a break to share a cold beer on the posh upper deck of the fancy yacht. We didn't know what to call the thing. It had no name on the transom. It was Florida registered but not Coast Guard documented. There were no customized items aboard with the boat name on them. It had zero personality as far as I could tell. Azimut was an Italian yacht builder. The name translated into azimuth in English, which was the angle of an object in the sky in relation to a compass reading. If a celestial body was due north, it had an azimuth of zero degrees.

"So what do we call this otherwise nameless, faceless, absurdity of a vessel?" I asked Brody.

"Azimuth. Something to do with the sky," she said. "Something heavenly."

"What's Italian for celestial?" I asked.

She quickly looked it up on her phone.

"Celeste," she said. "I like it."

"Celeste it is then," I said. "I'll get a decal made up as soon as we get to the marina."

"At least we accomplished one thing today," she said.

"I'm making progress," I said. "But I've had enough for one day."

"Me too," she said. "I'll try some more tomorrow."

"After we move these boats," I told her. "No point in delaying our departure."

"I'll call the marina and get a slip for *Miss Leap,*" she said. "You sure this big boat will fit in the Don Pedro anchorage?"

"It's six-feet at low tide," I said. "That gives us a whole foot to play with."

"You're the captain."

Brody had learned well about operating our old trawler. The twelve-mile run from Pelican Bay to Don Pedro Island would be a snap for her. I asked her to idle around in circles while

I anchored *Celeste*. I'd tow the dinghy and use it to join her on *Leap of Faith*. We'd continue to the marina, retrieve our car, and begin stocking up on supplies.

We had a few more beers as the sun set over the mangroves of Cayo Costa.

"I've got two organizations lined up to help us distribute the goods," said Brody. "We're going to Cabo Rojo, on the west coast."

"That's near Boqueron," I said. "I stopped in there a long time ago on one of my jaunts to the BVI."

"Just north of there," she said. "I was told that Marina Pescaderia could accommodate us."

"Who are we meeting up with once we get there?"

"Light and Hope for Puerto Rico," she said. "It's a group of young people who know the actual conditions on the ground. They've been coordinating with various aid groups from around the world. I also have a church that needs help, Cuidad Refugio."

"City of Refuge," I said. "Sounds appropriate. Good work."

"Now we just load this ship to the gunnels with goodies," she said. "You get us there and I'll get it to where it will do some good."

"Teamwork," I said. "You and I make a good team."

"We do seem to complement each other," she said.

"It will be nice to accomplish something helpful instead of battling the bad guys," I said. "I'm looking forward to it."

"I'm proud of you," she said. "This may be a turning point in our lives. It will be nice to have a purpose."

"I'll try it on for size," I said. "See if it agrees with me or not."

For years I had no purpose, other than to survive. I eventually got ahead of the game financially, though by illegal means. I did a good job avoiding responsibility after that. All I cared about was the next sunset or the next walk on the beach. My purpose was to simply exist in peace, away from the outside world. I liked it that way. Then came Holly. Our partnership demanded a certain amount of responsibility, but we avoided it as much as possible. We dawdled away our days on remote island beaches. It wasn't enough. We got restless, each in our own way. We sought out adventures. We struggled to find our purpose. In the end, we decided that we wouldn't find it together. She went off to make her own way and I found Brody. Actually, Brody found me, but that's another story. Since we'd joined forces I'd willingly made some changes in my outlook. I was happy to adjust my life to accommodate her. I'd fallen into some projects that were fulfilling to us both. We'd helped people in our own unconventional way. Bailing out an aging dope smuggler by helping him sell some of his product and taking the rest off his hands wasn't exactly your typical charitable act, but we'd bailed out someone in need. The extra weed went to a veteran's group, for medicinal purposes of course. We killed two birds with one stone during that ordeal.

Now we were stepping up our game. By some odd karmic coincidence, our kind deeds were rewarded with a big-ass yacht. We fully intended to turn that stroke of good fortune into aid for others. Maybe I was redeemable after all.

The next morning I anchored *Celeste* in Kettle Cove, just behind Don Pedro Island. We took *Leap of Faith* into the marina. Our car started right up and we drove around trying to find a pontoon boat to rent. The first place turned us down because we had no credit card. I threw a pile of cash at the second guy and he took it. We argued a bit about keeping the boat overnight for a few days, but another hundred dollar bill swayed him.

"I'll bring it back in fine shape and full of gas," I promised him.

We parked the pontoon along the wall near the dry storage area. We didn't ask permission, we just did it. We took a look at our wish list of supplies.

"Batteries seem easy enough," I said. "Let's start with that."

"Walmart," she said. "I'll get a cart full of diapers and you load up with batteries. Meet me at the self-checkout."

We wheeled our two full carts up to the register. I'd rounded up every battery in the store. My cart was overflowing. Brody had diapers stacked six feet high. We got strange looks from the attendant. We got two more carts to help us scan everything through. We simply picked up an item, scanned it, and loaded it into the next cart. When it came time to pay the machine didn't want to take our cash. We had to get the attendant to resolve the matter. Damn machines.

That first load filled the car up pretty good. There was no room to go back in for more. We drove back to the marina and loaded it all into the pontoon. There was plenty of room aboard for more. Back to Walmart we went. We emptied the shelves of feminine hygiene products and first aid supplies. I had a cart full of bandages, gauze, tape, peroxide, antibiotic cream, etc. Brody had every shape, style, and brand of lady stuff you could imagine. We got more strange looks from the attendant, but our system was a little smoother the second time around. This carload took up the rest of the space aboard the pontoon boat.

We drove out to *Celeste* and unloaded our cargo. Most of the day was gone. Inside the big boat, our pile looked quite small. We had room for a dozen more loads. This was going to take longer than I had originally thought. We made one more run, this time to Home Depot. They had six portable generators in stock. I bought them all. They had a dozen big tarps, but not big enough to cover a roof. I bought them anyway. The car was full. By the time we unloaded again, I'd had enough for one day. Our haul still looked puny in the cavernous interior of the Azimut.

We revisited the list and made a plan for the next day. We got an early start in order to maximize our time. Since our legal problems had been resolved and we were no longer wanted by any law enforcement, Brody had purchased all the devices that everyone seems to depend on these days. She had the latest smartphone and a new iPad to go with it. She identified Tractor Supply as the best option for big tarps. They also sold generators. We made it our first stop. They had a nice supply of heavy duty tarps. We took them all. We picked up three more generators. They weren't a brand name but we didn't figure anyone would care. The car was quickly filled to the ceiling. The trunk wouldn't close but we drove it down the road anyway.

We offloaded into the pontoon and then again into the big boat.

"What next?" I asked.

"Solar stuff," she said. "Chargers and lights. We should find battery operated fans if we can too."

"West Marine," I said. "Luci Lights will be great."

"Let's go."

First, we drove to Venice to the nearest West Marine. They had ten solar lights and a handful of solar charging devices. We bought everything they had. It didn't fill a grocery bag. We made the decision to drive to Port Charlotte. That store had roughly the same supply, which we promptly bought. The next stop was in Punta Gorda. We bought them out of solar lights and chargers as well. On the way back, we stopped at Lowes and bought a cart full of cheap solar yard lights. All of it was transported out to *Celeste*. Once again, most of the day was gone. There was still plenty of room for more stuff.

"What do we do now?" I asked.

"We still need flashlights, lanterns and a few other items," she said. "Then we double up on some of the stuff we've already bought."

"We took everything on the shelves," I said.

"There's more than one Walmart around here," she said. "Hardware stores too."

"This is taking forever," I complained.

"Patience," she said. "There's no point in making the trip with a half-full boat."

"You're right," I admitted. "Let's make another run tonight before we call it quits."

We drove to Murdoch and went into another Walmart. I loaded my cart with flashlights, camping lanterns, and more batteries. Brody got more diapers. After putting it all in the car we went back for more. Brody got lady stuff and I got first aid supplies. We jammed it all in the car as best we could and headed back to the marina. By the time we finished stowing it all, I was worn out. I got us each a beer. We sat down and caught our breath.

"You know, the bed on this boat is a lot bigger than what we have on *Miss Leap*," I said. "What do you say we christen it and stay here tonight?"

"You sure you're up for it?" she asked.

"Get out of those clothes and I'll show you," I said.

She dropped her clothes on the floor, making a trail to the stateroom. I lived up to my end of the bargain.

We had to drive even further the next day to find more supplies. We had the routine down though, and each stop went smoothly. The salon and side cabins on the Azimut were nearly full. We saved just enough room for our own needed provisions. Our next to last stop was at the grocery store for food and drink. Our last stop was at the liquor store. The boat was loaded.

I topped off the pontoon with gas and returned it. Brody picked me up and we treated ourselves to a nice dinner at the Placida Grill. We made arrangements with the dock master to bring the Azimut in for diesel the next morning. It would be a tight squeeze, and I didn't need other boats taking up space on the fuel dock.

We buttoned up *Miss Leap* in preparation for our departure. I assured her we'd be back soon. She didn't seem too happy about being left behind. I knew that she'd be better off in the marina than out at anchor. No one would mess with her there. Neighbors would keep an eye on her.

I spent the evening getting familiar with the electronics. I played with the GPS, plotting courses. It was tied into the autopilot, which meant that once engaged, it would make turns and course corrections for me. It was fancy stuff for a boat bum like me, but I intended to make full use of its capabilities. As long as we didn't run out of fuel, the trip would actually be fun.

Later that night, I lay awake worrying over all the things I'd neglected to do. I had no clue about the engines on *Celeste*. They were fairly new but looked completely foreign to me. I never was a diesel mechanic. If something went wrong I wouldn't know where to start. I hadn't bought extra fuel filters or changed the oil. I hadn't done most of the things that I always did before taking *Leap of Faith* on a trip. I scolded myself for the oversight. It was my job to make sure the vessel was ready, and I'd simply not done it. We'd have to take another day, at least, to do the proper maintenance.

I'd lost much of my hyper-awareness over the past months. It simply wasn't needed. Our troubles were all behind us. We'd lived a life of comparative luxury. We'd gone on no great adventures. We had all the money we'd ever need. We even had some friends. There wasn't much point in staying constantly alert for danger when floating in the pool or having drinks at sunset. That kind of vigilance will wear a man down. I could no longer justify any paranoia. No one was after me or Brody. I'd relaxed like any man should have. I enjoyed what life had offered me, especially Brody.

It was time to turn it back on. The open ocean was nothing to take lightly, big boat or not. Puerto Rico, though technically part of the United States, was largely third world. Outside of San Juan and the resort areas, vigilance was required. The area we'd be visiting had been hit hard. Some folks might be desperate. Brody found me cleaning guns in the salon.

"What are you doing up?" she asked. "Big day tomorrow."

"We're going to have to delay our departure," I said. "Bunch of maintenance to do. Some other shit to work out. Sorry."

"I see you flipped the switch," she said. "I can see it in your eyes."

"Doesn't hurt to be prepared," I said. "This trip might be a joyride, or it might not."

"I have enjoyed your time off duty, Breeze," she said. "But I have to admit I almost missed this side of you. It's part of what attracted me to you in the first place."

"You'll have to stay alert too," I told her. "We're a team remember."

"I'll be ready," she said. "Now you've got my blood pumping."

"Well, we're both awake in the middle of the night," I said.

"May as well make the best of it."

Three

We found the owner's manual for all of the onboard systems. I spent the morning flipping through them and drinking coffee. I crawled around the engine room to further familiarize myself. I wrote down the model numbers on the fuel and oil filters. I found a maintenance log in a cabinet down there. The things I was worried about had all been serviced recently. All I needed was some backup filters, and some tools. We ran out to buy what we needed which took all afternoon to find. I also got two fifty-five gallon drums and a small transfer pump. I picked up some five-gallon jugs for diesel also. I called the dock master to reschedule our fuel stop. Everywhere I went, I kept my eyes and ears open. I watched the body language and posture of everyone I encountered. I sat and listened to the hum of the engines, searing the sounds into my memory. I felt her vibrations. I double checked every item on my checklist. Everything was in good working order. It was almost dark before I was satisfied that we were ready to go.

I decided that the best way to avoid any hangups at the fuel dock was to be there when they opened. If we tied up there for the night, we'd have access to the car for any last minute provisions we might need. We could also get to *Miss Leap* to pick up my tools or anything else we'd forgotten. I idled into the entrance channel just as the sun set over Palm Island. I laid *Celeste* up against the dock on her starboard side. Brody managed to grab lines and secure us without difficulty. Folks waiting for the water taxi gawked at our fancy yacht. Brody went to *Miss Leap* to round up a few things while I filled the water tanks.

Even though the office was closed, the dock master showed up to ask what I was doing there. I offered to pay the full transient rate for the night. He said we could settle up in the morning. I hadn't kept track of what this operation was costing us. I really didn't want to know. Just the first fuel fill up was going to run me a couple grand. Brody came back with some extra clothes and our toiletries. We'd obviously not gotten everything we needed. I sent a message to my brain to step it up a notch. I was out of practice.

We surveyed our cargo. Some of it wasn't secure, but diapers and tarps wouldn't hurt much if they shifted around. We had two staterooms and the bulk of the salon stacked high with goods. Our stuff was in the master stateroom. We left the settee open for meals and trip planning. I wished we could have loaded more, but we'd really used up all the available space. I was tired of shopping anyway. It was time to get the show on the road, or the water.

"We've done pretty well, Breeze," said Brody. "Don't you think?"

"As well as we could've hoped for," I agreed. "But I've had enough of checkout counters for a while."

"There's not a battery left in the whole county," she said, laughing. "Some stock boys are going to wonder what happened."

"Some mothers are going to wonder where all the diapers went," I said.

"We didn't empty the grocery stores," she said. "There will be plenty available."

"Just a temporary shortage," I said. "Everything will be restocked in a few days I'm sure."

"Have you got our routes laid out?"

"Marathon tomorrow," I said. "Then George Town in the Exumas, Grand Turk, the Dominican Republic and finally Puerto Rico."

"So five days?"

"Weather permitting," I said. "Let's look into that now."

Brody fired up her tablet and started opening weather apps. This was yet another thing we'd overlooked. My concerns were eased when she reported clear sailing for the next three days. The forecast was also good for the longer term, but nothing is reliable beyond three days. We'd be deep into the southern Bahamas by then.

I should have relaxed next to Brody with a cold beer and enjoyed the evening, but my mind was busy. I ran through the routes in my head, made endless fuel calculations, and worried about bad weather. I tried to leave the distribution of goods up to Brody, but I worried about that too. I didn't want to just dump off our stuff on a dock somewhere. I wanted to be sure it would go to those who needed it most. I ended up slugging down some rum to help me slow down. I drifted off to sleep soon after.

I was double checking our safety gear when the marina staff arrived in the morning. A nice young lady named Sandy said good morning. A very young kid named Mitch did the same. Mitch must have been the low man on the totem pole. He handled the chore of pumping out our holding tank while Sandy handled the fuel. Both of them were respectful and pleasant. The bill fell eighty dollars short of two grand. I told the two of them to split the change. They seemed appreciative. I wasn't used to tipping dock hands, but I'd never had this kind of money or this kind of yacht. Then I remembered the fee for overnight dockage.

"The boss said don't worry about it," said Sandy. "Anyone who buys this much fuel deserves to spend the night for free."

"Thank him for me," I said.

I realized I just enjoyed one of the perks of wealth. It didn't feel right, but I accepted his generosity.

I stood at the helm trying to figure out how to get off the dock. There wasn't enough room to back all the way off the dock. I'd hit shallow water and dig the props in the mud. Brody waited for my instructions after tossing off the lines. I eased back until the last dock piling was mid-ship. Using both engines and the bow thruster, I pivoted on that piling until we were lined up with the channel. The thin stainless rub rail prevented scratches on the hull. Mitch pushed us off with all his might. As soon as we were clear I shifted both engines into forward and eased away from the dock. The Azimut did six knots at idle speed. I left it there as we headed south in the ICW and all the way to the Boca Grande bridge. I kept an eye on the fuel flow gauge to get a feel for fuel burn at slower speeds and filed that information away for future reference.

Once we cleared the swing bridge, I brought her up on plane. She threw a mean wake and I was forced to constantly slow down when we encountered other vessels. I was relieved to exit the Boca Grande Pass and keep her running at twenty knots. I engaged the autopilot and let the sophisticated electronics package do its thing. Our bearing was due south. There wasn't much to worry about out here. Commercial traffic was non-existent along the west coast of Florida. We'd see a few shrimpers and crabbers. There were a few towers out there, but they were easily spotted from a distance. All that was left to do was relax in the air-conditioned bridge and enjoy the ride.

"Everything down there is riding pretty well," said Brody. "Weather still looks good. Where do we stay in Marathon?"

"We'll go into Boot Key and get fueled up," I said. "But we'll have to anchor outside. Get some sleep and run for the Exumas in the morning."

"Wow, two days to George Town," she said. "Hard to imagine going that far so fast."

"It will take sixteen hours from Marathon," I said. "Long day and we'll arrive in the dark."

"This thing practically drives itself," she said. "We can rest up on the way."

It seemed too easy. Piloting *Leap of Faith* to George Town took weeks. Was I missing something? Were my fuel calculations correct? Would the weather cooperate? I distracted myself from worry by making a visit to the engine room. All systems looked and sounded fine. The dripless shaft seals were dry. I sensed no unnecessary vibrations from the turning shafts. The engines hummed, wanting more fuel. They were built to go much faster, but I wanted to keep them reined in. I wanted to be one with the feel and sounds of them. So far, so good.

We pulled into Boot Key just after four o'clock that afternoon. We made it to Burdine's fuel dock before it closed and topped off the tanks. I made a three-point turn alongside the old Faro Blanco marina to aim us back out the channel. It had been abandoned for years, but it was even in worse condition after Hurricane Irma. A handful of wrecks were jammed into decrepit docks making it into a boat graveyard. We idled back out to the south end of Boot Key and anchored for the night. I sat back relaxing in the cool comfort of the salon, listening to the soft hum of the generator.

Then it hit me. The damn generator was burning diesel. I had no idea of its fuel consumption, but I certainly hadn't figured that into my calculations.

"We've got to shut everything down," I announced.

"Say what?" asked Brody. "Even the air conditioners?"

"The generator is stealing fuel," I said. "Even if it's only ten or twenty gallons per day, it could mean the difference between making it and running out."

"There goes our luxury cruise," she said.

"I'm sorry," I said. "But we don't have air conditioning or a generator on our boat. I just didn't think about it."

"I think we both need to clear the cobwebs a bit," she said. "How'd we get so lax?"

"All that easy living," I said. "It's to be expected."

"But I like the easy living."

"Me too," I confessed. "But it's made us soft."

I went below to investigate the generator. It was an eighteen kilowatt Kohler. I climbed back up and asked Brody to look it up and figure out its fuel usage. It took a while but she found it. At half load, it burned one gallon per hour. Overnight we'd lose ten or twelve gallons of fuel. During our sixteen hour trip to the Exumas, we'd lose another sixteen gallons. I simply couldn't risk running it to support the air conditioners. It was going to be a hot, sweaty night. I thought we could probably get away with using it once we fueled up in the Bahamas. The remaining legs were much shorter and we could get fuel in several places along the way.

"Temporary setback," I told Brody. "One night, maybe two."

"I shouldn't complain," she said. "We've been through much worse."

"You could be sitting in the Everglades battling killer mosquitoes," I suggested.

"Never again," she said.

I shut it down and the world got real quiet. No generator noise or air conditioning sounds bothered the peace. We took drinks out on deck to look at the stars. A slight hint of a breeze cooled us. It was all good until we tried to lie down and sleep. The boat offered no ventilation. It was clearly intended to be a dock queen, with the air on all day every day. We ended up digging out two battery operated fans. We stole some batteries from our stash to power them. It was just enough to keep us from suffocating. Neither of us slept much.

We gave up before daylight and went to put on some coffee. The coffee maker was a regular household model. It wouldn't work without running the generator. I realized that the stove was the same way. At least the refrigerator ran off the boat's battery bank. There was no inverter.

"Fifteen minutes," Brody pleaded. "What's that? A quart of fuel? We'll make coffee and I'll fix some breakfast."

I gave in and fired up the generator. The A/C vents blew out cool air. The coffee maker gurgled. The smell of bacon wafted out of the galley. Between flipping bacon strips, Brody stood in front of a vent and let the coolness cover her. I waited for the eggs to be done before shutting it all back down. The food and coffee helped to overcome our disappointment. At least we'd get an early start.

I started the big engines and raised the anchor just before daylight. We headed east, directly into the rising sun. The seas were calm and the air was hot. The bridge quickly became a greenhouse. We opened what windows we could, but it was still quite warm. Brody brought up the little battery powered fans. I concentrated on keeping *Celeste* at just the right speed for maximum fuel efficiency, but in a manner that would allow us to get there in a reasonable time.

The Gulf Stream tried to push us too far north. We lost some time and fuel fighting it. Once on the banks, I sensed a light westerly flow. It wasn't much, but it extended our estimated time of arrival slightly. I constantly made new calculations in my head. With what little we had in reserve, we should have been able to make it. We continued cruising along at twenty knots. That evening we picked up a light breeze, which helped to cool us off but hurt our forward progress. I had to advance the throttles to keep us on plane. The fuel flow gauge told me we were now burning fifty-five gallons per hour. I played around with the trim tabs and the throttles, trying to coax as much efficiency as I could out of the big yacht. It just wasn't built for conservation. For most of that night, it didn't look like we had enough fuel, but the breeze fell off in the morning and the seas became flat. I was able to back off the throttles and still maintain my optimum speed. I grew weary of the constant re-thinking of fuel burn. I finally gave up. Either we'd make it or we wouldn't.

At ten the next morning we passed the southern tip of Great Exuma. Long Island was off to starboard. The fuel gauge read empty. We made it through the southern entrance to Elizabeth Harbor before the engines started to sputter.

"Start dumping those five-gallon jugs into the fuel tank," I yelled to Brody. "It's only a few more miles."

I backed off the throttles and slowed to eight knots. The engines smoothed out and continued to run.

"Five gallons in," yelled Brody.

She continued to dump diesel into the tank and the engines kept churning along. After running at twenty knots for sixteen hours, eight knots seemed awfully slow. I could see the anchored boats near George Town.

"Twenty gallons in," she yelled. "Are we going to make it?"

"Yes," I yelled back. "Almost there."

"Should I start pumping fuel out of the drums?" she asked.

"No, we'll make it," I said. "I'll do that once we get anchored."

"Cutting it close captain," she said.

"I warned you fair and proper," I told her.

"You weren't kidding."

We drifted into an open spot amongst the anchored boats and dropped the anchor. Relief came over me. The hard part of the voyage was behind us. The rest of the trip would be relatively easy, fuel-wise. We decided to venture into town to see what the diesel situation was. The first thing we noticed was the missing docks at the Exuma Yacht Club. Irma or Maria or a combination of both had completely destroyed them. From the dinghy dock, we walked across the street to the Yacht Club. They no longer sold fuel. Only the restaurant was open for business. There was a Shell station nearby, but it was impossible to get a boat to it. There was no diesel to be had in George Town.

Redboone's Cage had burned down and had not been rebuilt. We walked two blocks until we found the cruisers' new hangout. We learned that the closest fuel was at the Emerald Bay Resort and Marina, about fifteen miles up the island. We had no choice but to use our spare diesel and motor up there to fill up. We went through the process but lost another day to the delay.

"How far to the next stop?" asked Brody.

"Two-hundred and fifty miles tops," I said. "We'll have fuel to spare if we stop in Providenciales instead of Grand Turk. From there it's two-hundred and forty miles to Samana on the east coast of the DR."

"Two perfect legs for this boat," she said. "You've done your homework."

"And we can run it all during daylight hours," I said. "Piece of cake."

We left at sunrise the next morning. After departing Elizabeth Harbor, we jogged around Long Island and set a direct course for The Turks and Caicos. Not having to worry about running out of fuel allowed me to throttle up just a bit. We ran in the mid to low twenty-knot range all day, shortening the trip by an hour or more. There were several marinas available to us, but we selected Blue Haven because Brody liked the name, and it was the newest facility out of the bunch. I was surprised by the number of massive luxury yachts tied up in the slips. The Azimut was the smallest vessel there, and the least expensive. Still, the staff treated us like royalty. We fueled up, took on water, and ate a nice meal.

"Too bad we can't hang out here for a while," said Brody.

"It's nice but I don't think we'd fit in," I said. "Maybe with some of the crew members."

"We've got a mission to fulfill anyway," she said. "Maybe we can stay a few days on the way back."

"Haven't given it much thought," I said. "We've got to do something with this boat when we're done with it."

"If we keep it much longer it's going to be hard to part with," she admitted. "It's actually pretty damn nice if all this stuff wasn't piled up in it."

"I figure the dead guy's widow will come looking for it sooner or later."

"Then what?"

"We haven't officially transferred ownership," I said. "Just give it back to her I guess."

"What if she doesn't come for it, or even know about it?"

"I don't know," I admitted. "It's a white elephant. Whoever puts it in their name will have to pay the tax on it. It needs a big slip which is expensive. The fuel bills are ridiculous. I don't know what to do with it."

"Can't we sell it without putting it in our name first?"

"It would take a slick broker to pull that off," I said. "But there's probably someone that would be willing. Miami or someplace like that. Sell it to a cartel boss."

"That's no good," she said. "We're supposed to be doing something good with it."

"Keep thinking on it," I said.

It was a two-hundred and forty-mile run to Samana. It would have been quicker to stop in Luperon, but diesel had to come out by barge and there was the off chance I'd run into an old lover there. I thought it best to skip it. We tied up at Puerto Bahia to take on fuel again. The only slips that they had available weren't quite big enough for our vessel, but they agreed to let us stay for one night. It was a challenge to slip *Celeste* into the narrow dockage they assigned to us, but I managed not to tear anything up.

"Good job, captain," Brody said. "You're getting pretty good with this thing."

"It's actually easier to dock than *Miss Leap*," I told her. "It's bigger but I've got more control with twin engines and a bow thruster."

"What's the next leg?" she asked. "Puerto Rico right?"

"A mere hundred and forty miles to Puerto Real," I said. "That's the bay where the marina is. Cabo Rojo is inland."

"I'll check the weather," she said.

"I'll go make us a dinner reservation," I said. "Let's get cleaned up and go eat something fancy."

After dinner, we made good use of the big bed in the master stateroom. The air conditioning chilled the air so our movements were under a big comforter. We were in the lap of luxury, enjoying the high life. Neither of us ever thought we could experience that kind of life. It wouldn't last forever at the rate we were spending money, but I had to admit it was a very nice change of pace. Brody soaked it all in.

"Wouldn't it be nice to live like this permanently?" she asked.

"If we had this every day we'd take it for granted," I said. "We'd probably start looking for an even nicer boat."

"Don't get me wrong," she said. "I appreciate our life on *Leap of Faith*, but this is just so fantastic."

"Consider it a vacation," I told her. "Our real home is waiting for us to return."

"I'll try not to be too disappointed," she said. "But remember our conversations about getting a bigger, nicer boat. Here's one that just fell into our lap for free. It's a sign maybe."

"I take it as a sign to pay it forward," I said. "Otherwise I'd have never taken the boat in the first place."

"We are paying it forward with this mission," she argued. "Maybe we could run more missions like it. Help more people."

"We'd run out of money," I said. "On *Miss Leap,* we can probably live forever on what we have."

"That's an important point," she said. "But I think we can find a compromise somewhere."

"Fair enough," I said. "Let's get this done and figure out what to do with this boat first, then we'll explore our options."

Four

The trip across the Mona Passage to Puerto Rico was a snap. We made it in five short hours on calm seas. I'd seen those waters boiled up and dangerous on previous trips, but the Gods smiled on us. Marina Pescaderia, as the name implies, was the fishing center of the west coast of Puerto Rico. Fishing vessels big and small lined the docks. The place was in fine shape. Most of the docks looked recently replaced or rebuilt. The buildings sported fresh paint. I found it interesting that a private enterprise could rebuild so quickly; while we were there to bring needed supplies to people the government couldn't restore electricity to.

I began a thorough inspection of the boat's various systems while Brody went to straighten out our cell phone situation. It turned out that our phone would work in Puerto Rico, as long as we were near enough to a tower. It worked well in the marina. She called the church first. Someone would come the next day to meet with us. She called Light and Hope for Puerto Rico. They too said they'd come to the marina in the morning. It looked as if we'd be free of our cargo in no time.

I sat and thought about the trip back. It would be nice to loiter in the islands for a while, but I was afraid that Brody would grow too attached to *Celeste* if we didn't get back to *Leap of Faith* soon. I also worried about the last long jump from the Exumas back to Florida. We'd barely made it on fuel coming over. Going back and forth to Emerald Bay for fuel added thirty miles to the trip. Any weather or course deviation would certainly cause us to run out of diesel. I sat down with the charts and the fuel flow information that I'd logged along the way. I determined that our best bet was to run at trawler speed. At seven or eight knots we'd make it on fuel, but it would take forever, almost two full days running non-stop. Both our boat and her crew were capable and it seemed like the safest option.

Meanwhile, we still had work to do in Puerto Rico. We had loaded all the supplies via the swim platform. That wouldn't work here. It all had to go over the side. We had no steps or boarding ramp to facilitate the process. It would be tedious and labor intensive. I decided to grab a beer and think it over. I hadn't drunk a sip of alcohol in days. That first cold one was well deserved in my opinion. After I was sufficiently relaxed and lubricated, I walked up to the office to see if we could enlist some help. I explained the situation to the dockmaster.

"I would happy to assist you," he said. "I'll have my men help. Just say the word."

"Much appreciated," I said.

"It is I who appreciate what you are doing," he said. "It's the least I can do. The people of Cabo Rojo will appreciate it as well. Are your contacts bringing trucks?"

"I don't know," I said. "I guess we'll see in the morning. We can stay as long as it takes to get everything distributed."

"You are welcome as our guests for as long as you wish," he said. "I'll see we discount your fees."

Two sisters from the church showed up first. Maria and Isabella were dressed in full nun regalia. They drove what looked like a military surplus truck. It would probably hold everything we'd brought. I carefully explained that some of it had to go to the other charity we'd contacted. They knew of them and approved. The two nuns walked through the boat and took stock of its cargo. They asked for a few generators, feminine hygiene products, and diapers. Maria said that the tarps, lights, and batteries were more needed elsewhere.

Three men from the marina showed up to help us. The truck was positioned as close as possible to the boat. Brody and I handed off packages to the nuns, who handed them off to a guy on our boat, who handed them off to the guys on the dock. The nuns sweated through their habits and didn't complain. It was way too hot to be working with all those clothes on. The marina's men were fit and strong. They took the job seriously and before we knew it, the truck was loaded with the nun's share of the loot.

"God bless you, Mr. Breeze and Miss Brody," said Maria. "The meek shall inherit the earth. May you inherit the seas."

"I'll drink to that," I said, reaching for a cold beer.

We wrapped up our goodbyes and I sat down to rest a bit. Just as I put my feet up, a couple from Light and Hope arrived. They were driving a Jeep with an extended bed. It wouldn't hold all that we had left. Marcos was nearly six-feet tall with broad shoulders and wavy dark hair that fell over his eyes. Evita had flowing long brown hair almost to her waist. She wore a floppy hat, worn jeans and work boots. Both were young and lean. Both were very serious individuals. They were a far cry from the millennial hipsters I always saw in Florida.

"Thanks for coming," I said. "You'll need to make several trips in that rig. We've got lots of stuff for you."

"Can I offer you a drink?" asked Brody.

"Water please", said Evita.

"How much stuff?" asked Marcos.

"Come inside," I offered. "See for yourself."

We made a quick tour of the boat. I could see by their expressions that we'd brought the right type of supplies.

"This will all be a big help," Evita said.

"We get so much useless stuff," said Marcos. "Kids' games, crayons and such. Tons of clothing. We can put all this to good use."

"Glad we could help," I said.

"Now we have to figure out how to get it all up to Cabo Rojo," said Evita. "This is more than we anticipated."

"The sisters at Cuidad Refugio have a big truck," Brody chimed in. "Breeze and I will pay for fuel."

"Can't hurt to ask," I said. "We brought this stuff all the way from the west coast of Florida. We'll do whatever we can to see that it gets distributed."

"You've done so much already," said Evita. "I will go and talk to the sisters."

As we walked backed to their Jeep, I noticed a group of potential troublemakers watching from the fish cleaning station. They were paying too much attention to our movements and talking low amongst themselves. *Celeste* was the most expensive looking vessel in the marina. I wondered if those guys thought we'd be an easy target for theft. I poked Brody with an elbow and nodded towards the young men. She acknowledged with an almost imperceptible nod while continuing to make small talk with Evita.

"If you can use the sister's truck," she said. "We'd like to go with you for a day or two."

"If it's not too much trouble," I said. "I can drive the truck. We can sleep in it if necessary."

"It's probably drier than some of the homes we'll be assisting," she said. "Those tarps will come in handy."

We all shook hands and they drove off towards town. Our thug buddies continued to show interest in our activities.

"You carrying?" I asked Brody.

"No," she said. "In my purse in the main salon."

"Mine is in the master stateroom," I said. "Board quickly and go straight for your weapon."

I didn't like the looks of the dockside gang. They didn't look like the typical American street gangbangers, but they did look rough. I didn't see any Latin Kings tattoos or gold teeth but my gut said they were trouble. No marina staff made a move towards them or said a word. They did, however, make a move towards us.

"Go, Brody," I said.

She jogged ahead of me and climbed aboard. I made it just ahead of our pursuers. As they approached the boat, Brody appeared with her weapon raised. I went in past her and retrieved my gun.

"Leave or die, assholes," she said.

I came to her side and pointed my weapon at them too.

"Or you can die first," I said. "We'll see that you leave afterward."

The apparent leader raised his hands in the air. The rest stood firm and crossed their arms.

"We didn't come to rob you man," he said. "Word on the street is you got relief supplies. Aid and shit."

"That's true," I said. "And we're determined to get it where it's needed most."

"We were just looking for a few tarps for my momma's house," he said. "Maybe some flashlights and batteries. I swear we don't mean no harm."

Was my gut instinct wrong about these guys? Did they need help for momma? Was this a ruse to gain access to the interior of our boat? I thought about sending them to see the sisters, but they hadn't taken any tarps. I realized that if we made enemies with this crew, our boat would be a sitting duck after we left with Marcos and Evita. I needed to negotiate with them.

"You, come aboard," I said to the leader. "The rest of you stay where you are. Keep them covered, Brody."

I sized up the young man. He was thin but wiry. The veins in his arms were pronounced. I was bigger but I'm sure he was meaner and in better shape. I saw no evidence that he carried a weapon, but a knife would be easy to conceal. I monitored his body language as he boarded the boat. I sensed no immediate threat, so I allowed him entry into the salon. I kept the pistol in my hand.

"You ain't gotta be such a hard ass, man," he said. "We just looking for a little charity. Ain't that why you came here?"

"You're out of place at this marina in the middle of the day," I said. "You've got no jobs. None of the staff tried to run you off. I'm thinking you've been intimidating them. You some kind of gang?"

He laughed heartily like I'd told the world's funniest joke.

"We too poor to be gangsters, man," he said. "Wannabes maybe. We don't have no guns. Ain't no drugs around here. We got churches and nuns all over the place though. Yea, we a gang alright."

"Your momma's roof damaged?" I asked.

"Ain't got no momma either," he said. "Me and my boys we shacked up in an abandoned house. Big part of the roof is gone. No electricity before the storms."

"How do you eat?" I asked.

"We work with the fishermen sometimes," he said. "When they can afford to pay us. Clean fish, paint boat bottoms, whatever we can scrape up. We hang out here a lot, trying to sniff out some work."

"Do you ever take advantage of the tourists?" I asked. "Pick pockets, steal purses?"

"Been known to happen," he admitted. "Sometimes we gotta do what we gotta do."

"You and your friends share whatever you earn or steal?"

"We buy food," he said. "Some liquor when we can."

My opinion of him changed, but only slightly. He'd rip me off if he saw the opportunity, but he wasn't as dangerous as I first thought. I offered him a deal.

"I'm going to give you what you need," I said. "And a chance to earn some money."

"What do we gotta do?" he asked.

"We're going up into the hills with the rest of this stuff," I told him. "You and your men watch our boat. Make sure nothing happens to it. It will be locked. I don't want you in it or on it. Just watch it from the marina and take whatever action is necessary to protect it."

"How much?"

"I'll give each of you a hundred now, and another hundred when I get back, provided she's safe and sound," I said. "If something happens to her, I'll find your little gang's shack and burn it to the ground with you in it. Understand?"

"Ain't giving up that hard ass act are you?" he said.

"It's no act, kid," I said. "I didn't get this far by being a pushover. You want the job?"

"Of course we want the job," he said. "I'll keep someone posted here round the clock."

I took him around and gave him four big tarps and some lights with batteries. After he handed them off to his buddies, I gave him a case of beer and a fifth of rum, not the good stuff. Their eyes lit up at the sight of the booze.

"Drink up tonight," I told them. "I want you sober while I'm gone. I'll get a full report from the dock master when I get back."

"Okay, boss man," the leader said. "You can count on us."

I handed each man a hundred dollar bill. Brody finally lowered her weapon.

"Your lady is a hard ass too," said the leader.

"She'll help me burn you out if it comes to that," I warned. "Probably pump a few rounds into your charred remains just for fun."

"Who the gangster now?" he said, laughing.

Maybe my rhetoric was a little over the top, but I wanted to express dominance. I'd been generous at the same time, a one-man good cop, bad cop. The tactic had worked for me before. We shook hands and they returned to their shady spot at the end of the pier.

"That's not how I expected that to go," Brody said.

"Me neither," I said. "Be prepared for anything. Adapt and adjust."

"You sound like one of my old FBI instructors," she said.

"Just stay alert," I said. "You sense anything out of the ordinary with that Light and Hope couple?"

"Not a thing," she said. "A little on the serious side, but they've seen a lot of misery."

Again, I tried to sit down and rest with a cold one. I almost finished with my first beer when

Marcos and Evita returned. This charity business was starting to feel like work.

"We can pick up the truck and load it in the morning," Marcos told us.

"Do you need a place to stay for the night?" Brody asked.

"It's not practical to return and then come back again tomorrow," said Evita.

"We can make room for you," I offered. "With half the stuff gone, we should be able to rearrange things to clear up a bed."

"Anyplace is fine," said Marcos. "I can sleep on the floor."

"You will not," said Brody. "Come on, Breeze. Help me move some of this stuff."

There would be no rest for the weary. We weren't finished with our mission yet, but I was ready for it to be over. I was ready to return to the easy life on Florida's west coast. I missed *Leap of Faith*. My benevolence had earned me two weeks of hard work and constant travel. I vowed to think twice before taking on another such mission. At least the big stack of diapers in the guest stateroom wasn't heavy.

Brody and Evita whipped up a fine meal for the four of us. We sat and talked about the current state of affairs in this region. San Juan was the center of activity and had received the bulk of the aid in the immediate aftermath of the storms. Ships lined the port and cargo planes jammed the airport. Electricity was restored there first. Once San Juan returned to civilized life, power and aid were slow to trickle out into the countryside. Warehouses full of bottled water and needed supplies sat baking in the tropical heat. The mayor of San Juan saw her opportunity to grab her fifteen minutes of fame. Her pissing match with the United States government did nothing to hasten the recovery. Contractors were flown in to restore the electrical grid. There were not enough trucks and supplies to attack the problems properly. The aging grid and the amount of devastation were too much. The heavily subsidized power company was broke and inefficient. Time marched on. The people who lived in the rural areas made do the best they could. Some were still making do without power, intact homes, or anything but the bare necessities for survival.

Marcos, Evita, and the rest of their group traveled constantly to the city to pick up and distribute whatever goods they could beg from whatever government official or aid worker they could speak to. They took in just enough donations from abroad to buy fuel and food for themselves. They'd filled out endless paperwork requesting grant money. They prayed for additional resources. Very little came their way. During some trips to San Juan, the load they returned with was worth less than the fuel cost. The more time that passed, the less help they got. The world had mostly forgotten about the poor in Puerto Rico. The big charities took in millions in donations in their name, but little of that money made its way to Cabo Rojo or any of the dozens of other affected rural areas.

"How do you keep it up?" Brody asked. "You must feel dejected at times."

"It is noble work," said Evita. "God's work. It is not a one-time mission for us. It is a lifetime calling."

"She did not mean to belittle what you've done," said Marcos.

"No offense taken," I said. "I only wish we could do more."

"What are your most immediate needs?" asked Brody.

"Short of having the power restored, our group could use a newer and bigger truck," said Evita. "We had a van but it died and we cannot get the necessary parts to make it run."

"And cash," said Marcos. "Donated goods are drying up quickly. We can't afford to buy supplies for our people."

Brody gave me a look. I knew what she was thinking. We had plenty of money and we could help these people more without any sacrifice. I took it under advisement. I wanted to get the goods up to the hills and distributed. I'd think more about how we could help further afterward. Evita seemed to sense the topic of our silent communication.

"You are very wealthy, no?" she asked.

"Yes and no," I said. "This yacht is not really ours, but we are free to use it as we see fit, at least for the time being."

"We have no use for a yacht," she said. "We couldn't afford the fuel."

"I didn't offer it," I said. "I was demonstrating that we may not be as rich as you assume."

"Still, you brought all of these goods and traveled all this way to help," she said. "Sounds like an expensive exercise."

"I wouldn't call it God's work," I said. "But it does have a certain nobility about it. We just wanted to do some good in this world."

"Do you do this sort of thing often?"

"Actually, no," I confessed. "I'm making an effort to atone for my sins."

"Kindness towards others will go a long way in that regard," she said. "You're a curious case, Mr. Breeze."

"Why do you do what you do?" I asked.

"Everyone should have a purpose in life," she said. "This island is not a land of great opportunity. The need is so great. I felt the call of duty and service to others."

"Like the sisters at Cuidad Refugio," I said.

"They tend to reserve their charity for Catholics," she said. "Not to dishonor their good deeds."

"So you fill the void that they leave," said Brody. "Help those the church can't."

"Or won't," said Marcos.

The conversation was getting a little deep for my tastes, and I was too tired to participate any longer. Brody rounded up pillows and blankets for our guests. I was asleep before she got in bed. Dreams from my past returned to torment me. My wife, Laura, was in a hospital bed. I couldn't get to her. Bobbie Beard was at my feet, battered beyond repair. Blood dripped off my knuckles onto the dirt where he lay dying. Laura appeared again. She was on the other side of a crumbling bridge. I tried to cross, but the bridge surface fell away under my feet. I hung from a trestle a thousand feet above the raging river below. Laura was gone. Bobbie came back. He was challenging me, questioning my manhood. He taunted me in front of Holly.

Brody shook me awake. I was thankful for the dreams to be interrupted.

"You okay?" she asked. "Bad dreams again?"

"I don't know, why," I asked. "I haven't had any dreams in a long time. I thought that was over with."

"What's been on your mind?" she asked.

"What we're doing here isn't enough," I said. "I know we can't save the whole damn island, but I need to help on a grander scale. If I'm ever going to swing that karma thing to the good, I've got to go big."

"Charitable work shouldn't be for selfish purposes," she said. "You want to help others to save your own sorry soul?"

"All charity is for somewhat selfish purposes," I countered. "It makes people feel good about themselves. Like Evita said, helping others goes a long way towards atonement."

"So what do we do?" she asked.

"Find a buyer for this boat, right here in Puerto Rico," I suggested. "Take the money and give it all to the Cuidad Sisters and the Light and Hope couple. Help them get a truck and whatever else they need."

"How do we get home," she asked.

"There must be an airport somewhere around here," I said. "Fly back and get on *Miss Leap*. Get things back to normal."

"And count your karma credits," she said.

"Something like that."

I managed to grab a few more hours of sleep without fighting through any more dreams. Evita and Marcos had already left to pick up their truck. I grabbed a quick bite and went to give a heads up to the dockmaster. My new security team was in their normal spot so I stopped to say good morning.

"What's your name, anyway," I said to the leader.

"Guillermo," he said, "But everyone calls me G."

"Just G?" I said. "Guillermo is Spanish for William isn't it. Why not Bill?"

"The Spaniards butchered the name and its meaning," he said. "First it was German for faithful protector."

"You made that up," I said.

"I shit you not, man," he said. "Look it up."

"Okay my faithful protector, G," I said. "Come with me to speak to the marina boss."

I explained what the plan was. G and his buddies were keeping an eye on *Celeste* until we got back.

"I assume you've left no valuables behind," said the dock master.

"It's all locked up," I told him. "They aren't to go aboard. Just sit there in the shade and watch over it. I'm paying them for their time. I think we've come to an understanding."

"Very good then," he said. "They aren't bad young men. They've just seen some desperate times lately. Work has been scarce since the hurricanes."

I handed the dock master a hundred dollar bill, just like I'd given G and his friends.

"You'll be sure to keep an eye on her too," I said.

"It is my job to protect the boats here," he said. "You don't have to pay me for that."

"Keep it," I said. "Get the wife a new dress or something."

"Gracias."

Five

The trip out to the countryside was bumpy and dusty. The old truck had a cranky five-speed manual transmission that took some getting used to. Marcos had filled it with fuel before we loaded it with the supplies. The nuns told him that we could make the roundtrip without additional fuel if we took it easy. We arrived at the field camp for Light and Hope for Puerto Rico in the middle of the afternoon.

The main headquarters was a big green canvas tent that looked like it came from the Vietnam era. It reminded me of the television show MASH. Smaller pup tents were arranged in a semi-circle around its perimeter. A smoking old generator powered a refrigerator, lights, and multiple fans. A power strip was full of cell phone chargers. We were introduced to the rest of the team who made short work of unloading the truck. Marcos and I set up two of the smaller generators we'd brought to take over for the ancient and noisy one they had. The noise level decreased significantly.

We all gathered around a foldout table to look at a map and plan out the distribution of goods over the next few days. Various team members knew who needed what, who had infants, and whose need was most urgent. Dinner was a big pot of some kind of stew that was barely edible. Dipping crusty bread in it was the only way I could get it down. Water was the only drink available. Cases of bottles were stacked in one corner of the tent.

The six team members were all in their twenties. They could have been students at any American University. They'd all left their homes and families to participate in the relief effort. I admired their selflessness. The only hint of modern luxury in that place was the row of cell phones charging. They'd obviously been resourceful. The command center was mostly surplus stuff like you'd find in an

Army Navy store. They spent most of their time taking turns on runs to San Juan for more supplies. They also took turns on the distribution runs. The Jeep could only carry so much. Two volunteers would drive out into the region handing out goods. They'd come back empty and another couple would take over.

Someone threw two sleeping bags at us and pointed to a vacant corner of the big tent.

"Sorry, we don't have any spare pup tents," they said. "We don't get guests up here."

"No problem," I said, wondering how my back would feel after sleeping on the ground.

The first load had already left when we woke up. Brody produced our toothbrushes and a tube of toothpaste. We used bottled water and spit on the ground out back.

"You sure know how to show a girl a good time," she said. "Yesterday a luxury yacht. Today a sleeping bag on the dirt."

"Makes you appreciate what we have," I said. "And what these kids go through."

"Money wouldn't be wasted here," she said. "They've done without long enough. I'm confident that whatever we can give to them will be put to good use."

"Me too," I said. "I've seen enough. Let's get that truck back to the church. See about selling *Celeste*."

"It will be tough to let her go," she said. "I really was hoping we'd find a way to keep her, but this is the right thing to do."

We went to talk with Evita before leaving. She went overboard thanking us. I asked how long the need would continue here.

"I'm afraid it will never end," she said. "They get tarps, but what they really need is a new roof. They get flashlights, but they really need the power restored. Another big storm and the cycle starts all over again."

"What will you do when you can do no more?" I asked. "When the money runs out and the donations cease?"

"Return home," she said. "Keep begging for grants and donations. Wait for the next catastrophe."

Brody and I looked at each other. I let her speak for us.

"I don't want to make a promise I can't keep," she began. "But we're determined to help your cause. I don't know how long it will take, but we intend to make a very generous donation as soon as we can."

"It won't go unappreciated," she said. "We will provide the best benefit with whatever you can give."

"Take this in the meantime," I said, handing her a thousand in cash. "We'll be back."

We filled the fuel tank before returning the old truck to the sisters. I thought they could use a new truck as well, but didn't mention it. Back at the marina, *Celeste* floated in her slip, apparently untouched. G was sitting in his shady spot alone. He had a busted lip and assorted scrapes and bruises.

"Get hit by a truck?" I asked.

"Some Netas came down from the city," he said. "We had to fight them."

"Netas?"

"An actual gang, man," he said. "They got on your boat. Two of my boys got hurt pretty bad."

"You fought a gang to protect my boat?"

"Faithful protector," he said. "Like I told you."

"I take it you won the fight?"

"We weren't winning," he said. "The dock boss came down with a gun and some dockhands. They ran them off."

"I'm really sorry," I said.

"How'd you know there was going to be trouble?" he asked.

"I didn't really," I said. "Just covering all the bases."

"We never had those Netas around her," he said. "You bring that fancy boat and they show up."

"I expect I'll be moving it out of here soon," I said.

"If not, then you fight them next time," he said. "And we'll take the rest of our money now."

"Of course," I said.

I handed him more cash then I'd promised. He and his friends had earned it. I went to thank the dock master too.

"I very much appreciate your defense of my property," I told him. "Sorry to bring trouble to your marina."

"It is not your fault," he said. "And I would have done the same for anyone. Your security team was fighting a losing battle."

"Who were these guys?" I asked.

"This gang formed in our prisons many years ago," he said. "It seems to be spreading to the streets, but we've not seen them here before."

"You think they came to specifically target my boat?"

"It appears that way," he said. "They didn't bother the locals, who don't have much to steal anyway."

"Then someone here tipped them off," I suggested. "You've got a gang sympathizer here."

"Hard for me to say who that may be," he said. "This is a new development for us."

"Might be best for me to move on," I said. "I don't want folks around here getting hurt on my account."

"Back to Florida?" he asked.

"Depends on what chance I might find of selling the boat in Puerto Rico," I said.

"You won't sell it here," he advised. "Best bet is the east coast. Puerto Del Ray has a thousand boats and several reputable brokers."

"I'd like to maintain contact with those Light and Hope folks," I told him. "Puerto Del Ray is a long way from here."

"Then Boqueron maybe," he said. "Big money there and lots of tourists when times are good."

"That would work," I said.

"There is a brokerage that specializes in large yachts," he said. "International clientele. I do not know them personally."

"Thanks for your help," I said. "Brody and I will leave as soon as possible."

"Keep your eyes open in the meantime," he advised.

"I always do."

I put Brody to work looking up marinas and brokers in Boqueron. It would be an easy day trip. I made sure we were topped off with fuel and water. I only made a cursory inspection of the other systems. With any luck, she'd be tied up at a marina in Boqueron and become someone else's problem before she moved again. Brody had grown to appreciate her, but I had not. Throughout our travels, she hadn't spoken to me once. I listened to her sounds but sensed no soul. She just didn't have what it took to be mine. I wouldn't miss her.

Brody picked Club Nautico for docking. There was a broker on site and several bars. I remembered anchoring there. It was the hotspot for young partiers on the weekends. The music had been loud and at times the shenanigans were obnoxious, but it had seemed a happy place. I reviewed the charts of the area as the engines warmed up. When I went to the helm, two dockhands arrived to assist Brody with the lines. G waved to us from his shady spot. I waved back, feeling guilty that we didn't share a better goodbye. I sucked at goodbyes.

The trip was a simple one. We entered via the northern channel, located the marina and called for a slip assignment. The docks were in reasonable shape, but the voice on the radio warned that they had no fuel. Hopefully, we didn't need any. After tying up we went to the closest bar to have drinks and listen to the local chatter. I'd observed that most brokers did a lot of business in waterfront bars, making contacts and closing deals. This place was no different. Within an hour a snappy looking American sat down with a file folder full of paperwork. His customer had some sort of European accent. The broker pointed and the buyer signed page after page of documents.

I waited for them to shake hands before making my approach. The buyer was happy with his new boat. The broker was happy with his commission.

"Excuse me," I interrupted. "Are you who I should see about listing my yacht for sale?"

"Indeed I am," the broker said. "The name's Ron. Ron Vendegna. Please, sit and have a drink. Tell me about your vessel."

I described *Celeste* to Ron and told him which slip we were in. He was obviously eager to make a deal. He paid for our drinks.

"There is just one potential small fly in the ointment," I said. "The ownership paperwork is questionable."

"How so?" he asked.

I told him exactly how we gained possession of the Azimut. He asked to see the documents. The three of us walked back to the boat and climbed aboard. Brody offered Ron a drink and he asked for water. I presented what little paperwork we had. He reviewed it and thought for a minute.

"Are you flexible on price?" he asked.

"I know what it's worth," I told him. "But I understand I may have to make compromises."

"Good," he said. "I think we're on the same page. I have a proposition for you. I've dealt with similar matters from time to time."

"I'm listening."

"We set up an LLC solely for the purpose of establishing boat ownership," he explained. "It's done all the time to hide the true owner's identity, or more often to evade paying taxes on the value of the vessel. Most choose the state of Delaware for that exact reason."

"No sales tax then," I said.

"Correct," he said. "We will take what you have to a lawyer tomorrow. He'll set up the LLC and you'll sign it over. I will sell it on behalf of the shell company."

"I'd like to make this quick if that's possible," I said.

"Selling an expensive yacht takes time," he advised. "Just the right buyer needs to be found."

"Will a significantly lower price speed up the process?"

"Possibly," he said. "How much lower?"

Brody stepped in with her tablet and showed him a list of similar vessels for sale around the world. They ranged in price from eight-hundred thousand to one million dollars. *Celeste* was in pristine condition with low hours on the engines. Her value was on the high end of the range. I could see the gears turning in Ron's head. His scratched his chin, deep in thought.

"Just how great is your desire for a quick sale?" he asked. "Consider what it is worth to you."

"What do you have in mind?"

"Don't be offended by what I'm about to offer," he said. "I'm just trying to help you out."

"I'm willing to negotiate," I said.

"I will buy your yacht tomorrow, right after we complete the paperwork, for five-hundred thousand."

"Make it six and you've got a deal," I said. "Still plenty of room for you to make a killing."

"I expected no less," he said. "Six it is. Pleasure doing business with you."

We shook hands to seal the deal. He recognized opportunity when he saw it. Who knows what sort of shady deals he'd been a part of over the years? I'd been lucky to find him. He'd been lucky to find me. I suspected he made his real living doing those types of deals. His commission would far exceed the normal ten percent. We arranged a time and place to meet in the morning. Brody and I went back to the bar to order dinner.

"I don't know what to say about what just went down," Brody said. "I want to be upset that we sold a million dollar boat for six-hundred thousand, but I'm pretty damn happy that we got that much for a boat that cost us nothing."

"Remember, we're giving it all away," I said.

"I'm so proud of you for that," she said. "The money is going to help a lot of people."

"Feels kind of nice," I admitted. "When we get back to the boat let's start figuring out how we're getting home."

Brody poked away at her tablet. I sat down and put my feet up, basking in the glow of good deeds to come. It would all be over soon. We could return to our regularly scheduled life in Florida. I promised myself to keep my eyes open for more opportunities like this one. It had made me feel good about myself.

"The Rafael Hernandez Airport is in Aguadilla," she said. "It's in the northwest corner of the island. Direct flights to Florida."

"How do we get there?"

"I don't know yet," she said. "There are no rental car companies around here."

"We need to make stops in Cabo Rojo and back at Marina Pescaderia."

"You're resourceful," she said. "Figure something out. Find a taxi or a bus."

I had a better idea. After we finished all the paperwork at the lawyer's office, I asked about buying a used car.

"Craigslist," said Ron. "Just like in the states."

He took us to the bank to convert our certified check into cash.

"You won't be able to travel with that kind of money," he said.

"We won't have it when we leave," I told him.

"Buying another boat?" he asked.

"No, we've got one waiting for us at home."

Craigslist Puerto Rico had dozens of cheap cars listed for sale. We made a few phone calls, settled on a 1985 Monte Carlo, and drove it to the boat to gather our belongings. The thousand dollar car looked comically out of place next to the million dollar yacht. Such was the life of Breeze.

We took our clothes, toothbrushes, and a suitcase full of cash back up the coast.

Six

The old Monte Carlo had seen better days. The air conditioning was lukewarm at best. The door hinges creaked and groaned. The shocks were shot. We bounced slowly up and down as we drove along. Brody laughed when I moved to adjust the rearview mirror and it came off in my hand. I tossed it into the back seat, adding to the collection of beer cans and burger wrappers already there.

We pulled into the field camp near Cabo Rojo, relieved to have made it without breaking down. We got curious looks at first until folks recognized who we were. Evita came to greet us.

"I didn't expect to see you back here so soon, if ever," she said.

"As you can see," I said. "We didn't waste our money on a fancy car, but we've brought you enough to get a new truck, among other things."

"I don't know what to say," she said. "We were discussing breaking down the camp and going home."

"No need to say anything," said Brody. "This is something we wanted to do. It's no real sacrifice on our part."

"You should be able to rent office space or build your own place soon," I said.

"You can't be serious," said Evita.

"Go get Marcos," I said. "We've got something to show you."

All of the Light and Hope volunteers gathered around our beater car. I put the suitcase on the hood and slowly opened it. I left exactly half a million dollars in it. The group stared in disbelief.

"It's real," I said. "Take it. Help your people. Live long and prosper."

Evita gave me a teary-eyed hug. Marcos hugged Brody. The whole group took turns hugging us both and thanking us profusely. Their gratitude was clearly genuine. I don't think I'd ever felt better about myself. I climbed the karma ladder a few more steps away from my past misdeeds. Brody's eyes sparkled with delight.

"Three cheers for Breeze and Brody," someone yelled.

"Wait," I said, putting up a hand. "I should be thanking you. It's difficult to explain, but you've given me the opportunity to make a real change in my life. Change doesn't come easy for me. Helping you has given Brody and me a great deal of satisfaction. I'm confident that the money will be used to benefit those who need help the most. I have complete trust that all of you will see to it. The money is freely given with no regrets."

"We appreciate your trust and your generosity," Evita said. "You're both angels. May God bless you and keep you."

"Amen," I said. "We're on our way. We've got some final business back at the marina."

"Vaya con Dios," said Marcos.

I turned the car around and we drove back down the dusty trail. Our next stop was Cuidad Refugio. We knocked on the door and asked for the two sisters. When they arrived, Brody handed them fifty grand. We turned and walked away without explanation. It was the only way to keep from lecturing them on helping everyone, Catholic or not.

We still had fifty grand to give away. We drove to the marina. The car didn't fall apart. The office was closed for the day, but G and his crew were drinking beer under the gazebo. We exchanged greetings. Someone handed me a beer.

"Where'd you get the clunker, man?" asked G.

"I traded the yacht for it," I joked. "Plus fifty grand."

I handed him the stack of hundreds.

"You fucking kidding me, right?" he said.

"You can have the car too if you want it," I said. "After you give us a ride to the airport."

"This is some kind of dream," he said. "Shit like this don't happen around here."

"It's for all of you," I said. "My advice is to get a decent place to live. Someplace where you can all find work. I'd rather you didn't blow it all on booze, but it's yours to do as you please. I'm grateful for what you did. Thank you all."

Each man came to shake my hand and say thanks. G was the last in line. I could see the water in his eyes.

"None of us ever caught a break," he said. "Life, man, it just never seemed fair. Maybe we can make a new start now. Thank you for your kindness."

"Life ain't fair," I told him. "Remember that. No one owes you shit. You've got to man up and keep on going. That's just the way it is. Take advantage of this opportunity. Don't quit when life shits on you again."

"He always talk this way?" he asked Brody. "Dude just spits it out, don't he?"

"He means well," she said. "We're both grateful for what you guys did for us."

"We'll be forever grateful to both of you," he said. "I mean that."

"Great," I said. "Now drive us to the airport. We've got a plane to catch."

"No offense," he said. "But I don't want that piece of shit. Drive it up there and leave it in the parking lot. Someone will steal it eventually."

"Suit yourself," I said. "But this means goodbye my friend."

"Goodbye, amigo."

All the money was gone. Our mission was complete. It was time to go home. We aimed our rattling, rolling jalopy north towards the Rafael Hernandez Airport. We were over halfway there when it started to overheat. We coasted into the parking lot of a roadside store. I raised the hood to let it cool down and went inside to see what I could find. I bought six eggs and a small tin of red pepper.

"What are you going to do with that?" Brody asked.

"Old farmers trick," I said. "Watch and learn."

I cracked the eggs and dumped them into the radiator opening. I emptied the full container of red pepper into the fill as well. I filled the radiator with water and started the engine. As the mixture circulated, the egg and pepper combination would lodge itself in the crack and seal it up, at least temporarily. I hoped it was enough to let us reach our destination. I kept a close eye on the temperature gauge. It ran a little hot but we made it to the airport. I parked it off by itself away from any lights, inviting thieves to steal it. I considered it one last act of charity before we left the island. The doors were unlocked and the key was in the ignition.

The number of flights was limited, but after a few hours wait we boarded a modern jet bound for Fort Lauderdale. A small commuter took us on to Punta Gorda. Brody called an Uber for the last leg of the trip to the marina. We were home. My heart lifted when I saw *Miss Leap*.

"It's okay, girl," I said. "We're back to take care of you."

"I swear," said Brody. "Sometimes I think you love this old boat more than you love me."

"I'd prefer to never have to choose," I said. "But let me say this; at this moment, I couldn't let you go for any reason. Certainly not for another woman, but not for a boat either."

"That's the most romantic thing you've ever said to me," she said. "I love you too, and I'd never force you to choose. It'll work out."

Her eyes did that sparkly thing, and in spite of our long journey, she never looked more beautiful. We postponed our showers until after sex. It was long, slow and completely satisfying. We got cleaned up and took cold beers up to the bridge to watch the sunset. It was good to be home.

We were content at last. I felt much lighter in my soul. I did a good thing, damn it. That could never be taken away. Brody had become to mean everything to me. Her support and guidance had made me a better person. I couldn't erase the bad things I'd done, but I could be better going forward. We settled back into marina life easily. It was nice to have unlimited access to electricity and water. We spent a lot of time at the pool. We took hot showers and went out to nice restaurants. We lived a life of leisure for almost a month.

Then Captain Fred called. Brody handed me the phone.

"It's time you quit goofing off, boat bum," he said. "I've got a job for you. Several jobs actually."

"I don't need the work," I told him. "But you know I'll help however I can."

"That's what I'm counting on," he said. "But you'll be paid handsomely."

"What's up, Fred?" I asked.

"I'm having a new yacht built," he said. "It's due out of the factory soon. I need you to go up there and take delivery of it for me."

"What kind of yacht?" I asked. "Where is it?"

"Hatteras," he said. "Hundred-footer. North Carolina."

"Where are you?"

"Columbia," he said. "Can't get away right now."

"I thought you'd quit wheeling and dealing after your big score," I said.

"A man needs something to do," he said. "Can't help myself."

"Where's this new boat going?" I asked. "No one around here has dock space for something that big."

"City of Fort Myers," he said. "At least temporarily."

"I can handle that," I said. "Brody and I will be happy to deliver her for you."

"That's just the start of it," he said.

"Right," I said. "Several jobs. What else you need?"

"You're my new security consultant," he said. "I want her outfitted with the latest and greatest technology."

"I don't know jack about that stuff, Fred," I said. "I rarely even lock my own boat."

"Go about hiring the experts," he said. "You oversee. Get a feel for the boat and make sure they cover all the bases."

"Brody will be a big help with that," I said. "We'll start doing some research."

"Atta boy," he said. "I knew I could count on you."

"When this vessel supposed to be ready?"

"Two weeks," he said. "But it's been pushed back twice already. If you can, go on up there and prod them along. Keep after them to get her splashed. Go on the sea trial."

"This whole project ain't going to be cheap," I said. "How do all the expenses get paid?"

"I'll overnight you a credit card," he said. "No limit. Keep your purchases to boat-related expenses, to include hotels and whatever else you need to get everything done. I trust you'll see I don't get ripped off."

"I've got my own money, Fred."

"I didn't mean you," he said. "I meant the yard, and whoever else you hire to do the work."

"Now I'm a general contractor," I said. "Breeze Marine Services."

"That sounds good," he said. "Get some business cards made up. We'll make you a fortune."

"Which would seriously interfere with my boat bum image," I told him. "Unlike you, I'm just fine with nothing to do."

"I figured as much," he said. "Take care of this for me and you can get back to ogling bikinis at the pool."

"Brody's the only one worth ogling," I said. "It ain't exactly spring break central around here."

"Glad to know you two are still getting along," he said. "There's hope for you yet."

"She's great," I said. "But she keeps hinting at a bigger boat."

"Why do you think I'm buying a hundred footer?" he asked. "Make her happy, son. I'll sell you *Incognito* cheap."

"I don't know," I said.

"Think about it," he said. "I'll make you a good deal. Maybe trade for services rendered."

"Has Brody been talking to you behind my back?" I asked. "Sounds like you two are plotting a scheme."

"I wouldn't tell if she was," he said, laughing. "I just think it would work out for all of us. I'll have to do something with *Incognito*. I don't want to own two boats."

"Thanks for offering," I said. "I'll consider it."

"Make sure you tell Brody," he said.

"We'll talk it over," I said.

I gave him the address to send the credit card. He said it would come via FedEx. He'd call the Hatteras people and let them know who I was and that I was on my way. Brody was thrilled with all of the news. She thought that she would enjoy being aboard a spanking new hundred-foot yacht. She was also intrigued by the prospect of acquiring *Incognito*. She offered unlimited sexual favors if we could get Fred's old boat.

"I thought I already had that particular perk," I said.

"Not if you say no," she said.

"I see how you are," I said.

We started packing for the trip right away. Brody booked us a room in New Bern, North Carolina. The factory was just up the Neuse River a bit. I wasn't very familiar with the area. Once again, I had to prepare *Leap of Faith* to be left alone for a while. She was not happy about that at all. We hadn't left the marina once since we got back from Puerto Rico. I felt guilty about it.

Our platinum American Express corporate card arrived and we drove off to start a new adventure. Food and fuel were now on Fred. The Hampton Inn was nice enough, but not overly fancy or expensive. We got a feel for the town and located the Hatteras factory before calling it a night. I was excited to see Fred's new yacht. Brody was excited to take possession of his old one.

"Can't you just picture me in a bikini on the bow of a seventy-footer?" she asked.

"Of course I can," I said. "But we'll have to find a new marina."

"Where can we go with a boat that big but still be close to where we are now?"

"Fort Myers or Fort Myers Beach," I said. "Or north to Long Boat or up the Manatee River."

"Palmetto, Bradenton area?" she asked. "I don't know if I'd like that."

"Long Boat is nice," I said. "A seventy-foot Hatteras would fit right in with the clientele. A bit stuffy for my taste though."

"First you found fault with any boat I was interested in," she said. "Now you're going to find fault with any marina that can accommodate us."

"Maybe you're right," I said. "My subconscious doesn't want to think about parting with *Miss Leap.*"

"Look," she said. "I get it. You two are joined at the hip. You loved her before you ever knew I existed. But she's old, Breeze. She was great to us, but we deserve more comfort and luxury, don't you think?"

"You deserve all the comfort and luxury that you desire," I said. "I'm fine with what I have. You know that."

"Are you saying we won't get a nicer boat?"

"We'll get the damn boat," I said. "If that's what you want. I want you to be happy."

"And I want you to be happy too," she said. "I'm sure you'd love it on a newer, better boat."

"You're probably right about that too," I said. "How do you manage to be right so often?"

"I only want what's best for us both," she said. "You're not used to considering the wants and needs of two people instead of just yourself."

"Guilty as charged," I said. "But I've been trying very hard to adjust my thinking."

"You've done a fine job," she said. "I won't pressure you anymore tonight, but sooner or later we're getting a new boat."

"Then it might as well be *Incognito*," I said. "It's a good boat."

She looked at me with love in her eyes and gave me a big hug.

"But I'm keeping *Miss Leap*," I said. "We'll have two boats."

Seven

The Hatteras folks were quite pleasant. We got a quick look at Fred's new boat and a tour of the facilities. I asked to meet with the project manager or whoever was in charge of putting the final touches on the new yacht. I made it clear that Fred wouldn't accept any excuses for further delay. I was assured that great attention was being paid to every last detail. When the vessel was finished, it would be flawless. I arranged to do a walk-through the following day.

I was overwhelmed by every aspect of the shiny new Hatteras. You could fit three *Miss Leaps* inside of it. At one hundred feet in length and with a beam of over twenty-two feet, it was simply massive. There were ample accommodations for a dozen people. Everything was better than first class. I was handed a stack of manuals to go through. I took a seat amidst all the luxury and browsed the information.

The twin engines gave her over three thousand, five-hundred horsepower. It would burn a ton of fuel, but it carried over forty-six hundred gallons of diesel. The water tanks held over eight-hundred gallons. The three separate holding tanks equaled over four-hundred gallons of capacity. The raised pilothouse made me feel like I was at the helm of the Starship Enterprise. It took me an hour to figure out what all the switches were for. The electronics package alone had to cost a hundred grand.

"I've never seen anything like it," Brody said. "What do you think it cost?"

"Ten million or more," I guessed. "Fred's got the money."

"Maybe he could buy another one and put it into charter service," she said. "Let us run it."

"I don't like people enough to be in that business," I said. "You know that."

"You just drive," she said. "I'll take care of the passengers. It would certainly take care of my itch for a bigger boat."

"I could never ask Fred to do something like that," I said. "It's his money. He can spend it how he sees fit."

"Just a thought," she said. "A dream really."

A quality control technician was still poking around checking all the systems. He was thorough. I didn't want to bother him, but I watched what I could without interfering. He was using a thick checklist to make sure nothing had been overlooked or finished in a less than perfect fashion. I was getting nervous about piloting the huge vessel. I was uncomfortable on the bridge. I felt like I was responsible for a ship, not just a pleasure yacht. "You'll be fine," Brody assured me. "This is what you do. You're a natural."

"I'm just going to take it real slow and deliberate until I get a feel for her," I said.

"By the time we turn her over to Fred, you'll be able to teach him how to handle it," she said.

"At least I'll be making myself useful," I said. "All this is on his dime."

"But it's our time," she said. "We're doing him a favor."

She was right yet again. It was obvious that we were the only people he could trust with this job. I'd done some good work for him over the years. A few of those jobs were confidential and extremely important to him. Prior to that, he'd helped me out whenever I needed it, no questions asked. When he felt that I'd done more for him than he'd done for me, he compensated me financially. It had always been a mutually beneficial relationship.

For the first time on the trip, I wondered if we'd encounter any danger. Fred had enemies. Did they know about his latest purchase? Did they care? Though I figured it was only a small possibility, I put it on my radar. We needed to be ready if one of Fred's corporate or underworld rivals tried to make a move on the Hatteras, even if it was just to plant listening devices. I knew that he had professionals sweep *Incognito* for bugs on a regular basis.

We'd both brought weapons, but they were still packed away in our luggage. I advised Brody to make hers more accessible. She didn't call me paranoid. She simply transferred the weapon to her purse. She gave me a look that acknowledged my call to alertness.

We arranged dock space for the big Hatteras for after the sea trial. I contacted a few local private detectives inquiring about bug detection. I found one that assured me he had the latest technology and was available when requested. In the meantime, we didn't mention our travel plans when aboard the boat or around the factory. I had Brody work on our itinerary back at the hotel. Not that many marinas could accommodate us along our route.

Brody's use of modern technology, and my acceptance of it surprised me. I'd always just flown by the seat of my pants. Of course, I rarely used marinas. It was cheaper and more private to anchor out. I double checked the anchoring system and ground tackle on Fred's new vessel. It seemed only adequate for settled weather, in my opinion. I didn't want to take a chance on putting her on the rocks somewhere, or on a beach. We'd stick to marinas as much as we could.

Finally, the day came to splash her. A swarm of mechanics and technicians descended upon her. The engines were warmed up and the thru-hulls were checked. The dripless shaft seals worked their magic. The generator was started. It had enough power to run a small city. Fluid levels were checked and rechecked. Gauges were monitored. It took most of the day, but eventually, they were all satisfied that their area of responsibility was good to go. We all met in a conference room and each man responded to questions about his inspection. When it was over, the leader of the team looked directly at me.

"It's a go," he said. "Sea trial tomorrow."

The engines were running when Brody and I arrived the next day. We were joined by a professional captain, the chief engineer and the team leader. It was a nice day for a boat ride. I stood near the captain as he worked the controls to maneuver us away from the dock. I watched his every move. The big boat responded to his commands and we were underway. Once out in the Atlantic, the captain opened her up and ran her hard for thirty minutes. The engineer kept a watch on the gauges for a while then went below to inspect the engine room. He came back with a positive report.

We ran her at different angles to the waves to see how it felt. We made wide circles. We stopped and backed up in the open ocean. I was given some time at the wheel to play around with the controls. It turned on a dime and reacted instantly to whatever command I gave.

"I can handle her," I told them.

"Take us back to the inlet," said the captain.

"But I'll have to dock her."

"No problem."

We slowed to a crawl as we entered the river. The captain took over and brought her gently alongside the dock. Again, I watched him closely. There were handshakes all around. The vessel was deemed fit. We could leave when we were ready.

Brody and I loaded provisions and our personal belongings. The investigator came to sweep for listening devices. He found none. We were ready to take off. After having a few minutes at the helm during the sea trial, I was a little less nervous. I was still careful though. I used very short bursts of the engines and thruster to slowly separate her from the dock. Thankfully there was no wind. Brody yelled to me when we were clear.

"Take her away, captain," she said.

I eased both throttles forward and we left a gentle wake as we departed the Hatteras facility. Everyone representing Hatteras had been nothing but pleasant and professional. Ten million dollars will get you outstanding service.

Running in the ocean was a pleasure. We could see waves but the boat wasn't bothered by them. Running in the Intracoastal was another matter. We were big and there was a lot of traffic. I was on the VHF constantly talking to other captains. We traveled slowly. It was nerve-wracking. Each afternoon Brody would instruct me as to our destination. Once docked, we'd eat a nice dinner at Fred's expense. I grew more comfortable operating the boat each day. I managed not to hit anything or do any damage.

We topped off with fuel in Miami. There wouldn't be any more marina stops until we reached Naples. We took Hawk Channel on the outside down to Marathon and went under the Seven Mile Bridge. We ran at a leisurely pace northward across Florida Bay. There wasn't a single glitch in the performance of the new Hatteras.

After one night in Naples, we were ready to run up the Caloosahatchee River to the Fort Myers City Yacht Basin. Fred had arranged for a long-term slip ahead of time. Brody called to get our assignment. I slowed to a crawl as we entered the basin. I could feel all of the eyes watching our beautiful boat arrive. This was the moment when some captains screwed up. They feel the pressure of the audience and lose confidence. Current or wind impedes them and they fail to adjust. I'd had enough practice by then to get a little cocky. I spun her quick and lined up with the slip. I backed her in quickly and stopped her just in time. There was no yelling or running around. The dockhands grabbed lines and tied her off with no difficulty.

"Damn, captain," one of them said. "That was pretty slick."

"Nice job, cap," another one said. "Impressive."

"What was that all about?" asked Brody.

"Just showing off," I said. "They were all hoping I'd crash."

"Well I wouldn't advise doing that again," she said.

"We're here now," I told her. "That part of the job is done."

We let Captain Fred know that we'd arrived safely. He put us right to work researching security systems. We spent the next several days on the phone and internet learning all we could about the various companies in the yacht security business. We settled on Phantom Services. Their system was called NAV-TRACKER. Through their proprietary GOST Apparition HD system, they utilized the same satellites used by the Department of Defense. They claimed 99.99 percent reliability anywhere on the planet, except the extreme poles. I could see no reason that Fred would visit either pole or that his enemies would pursue him there if he did.

They offered messages and tracking, a vessel monitoring and surveillance center, INMARSAT Satellites combined with global relay and ground stations. They provided asset recovery, on-site security, rescue extraction via helicopter, and secure transport. Fred's new Hatteras would be the smallest vessel they'd contracted to protect, but he could afford their services.

An advance scout would arrive first and get the lay of the land. Later, a team of technicians would handle the installation of the various sensors and cameras. Before signing off, they'd want the captain to undergo training on its use. They'd need backup contact information as well. Brody and I agreed to go through the training. We could school Fred when he returned from Columbia.

We felt confident that we'd chosen the best. There wouldn't be that much to do once work began, other than familiarizing myself with the locations of the various equipment. I'd offer my advice if and when it seemed appropriate. I'd gotten to know the new

Hatteras fairly well. It was much too posh for my taste. Of course, Brody absolutely loved it. Thank God it was far out of our price range.

I cringed at the thought of moving aboard *Incognito*. We couldn't keep two boats forever. I feared it would be the beginning of the end of *Leap of Faith*. Unfortunately, the problem resolved itself. It was not a happy resolution. Captain Fred called.

"*Incognito* is on fire," he said. "The Pink Shell just called me. It's too late for you to do anything for her now, but can one of you run down there and figure out what happened?"

"Why just one of us?" I asked. "Oh, and sorry to hear this. She was a fine vessel."

"I don't think they know about the new boat yet," he said. "That's one of the reasons I had you bring it around. But they obviously knew where to find the old boat. Bastards took a bit of revenge on me I suppose."

"So one of us needs to stand guard here while the other goes to Fort Myers Beach?"

"Sorry to spread you thin," he said. "But you two are my boots on the ground. Let me know what you find out. Don't worry about money. Rent a car. Get a room. Whatever you need to do, do it."

"We're on it," I said.

I'm ashamed to say I felt a bit relieved at *Incognito's* demise. Anyone in their right mind would have jumped at the chance to own her, especially considering the thought that Fred might have given her to us for free. I'd been given a reprieve. *Miss Leap* was still there for us. Brody was practically in tears.

"I'll go down there," she insisted. "I'm better at this sort of thing than you. You stay here and protect this ship."

I didn't argue. She'd figure out what happened and say her goodbyes to the boat that almost was. I'd stay put and stay alert for the bad guys who probably wouldn't come. I'd be better at dealing with the security installers anyway. We'd knock out both jobs and go back home. We could wait to see how Fred would take care of us later. It didn't really matter to me. The trip had been enjoyable. It couldn't have gone any better. Too bad we now had a catastrophe to mar our mission. No one had thought that his old boat was in danger. Whoever did it had nothing to gain, other than vengeance.

Brody had the rental car company pick her up and she left that afternoon. It was only an hour drive. She wanted to get there while any evidence was still fresh. She needed to ask questions while the events were still foremost on the mind of any witness. She reverted back to her professional demeanor in a flash. She was an agent again, just not for the FBI.

I secured all the entrances and put my weapon in a convenient spot. I called the marina and asked them to keep an eye open for anyone snooping around. I was the new boat. I couldn't count on my neighbors to recognize strangers that shouldn't be there. From the raised pilothouse I had a good vantage point. It was air-conditioned and comfortable. I stayed up there until dark. After dinner, I decided to sleep in the salon. It would allow me to better hear anyone trying to enter. I locked myself inside and dozed off with the gun at my side.

Nothing happened. No one came. Three more nights went by without a sign of trouble. The advance man for Phantom Services arrived and got to work. He was all business. He took video of our initial walk-through. He used a recorder to take notes about what he saw. He took lots of pictures. He didn't rush anything. When he was finished he promised to put together a plan and forward an estimate for the work and equipment he proposed.

Brody returned with disheartening news. It had been an explosive device. The bomb did a lot of damage, but the fire finished off the job. No one was hurt, but no one knew anything either. Not one person that she talked to had noticed anything suspicious.

"Fred needs to call his insurance company," she said. "They are going to want what's left of it removed as soon as possible."

"Not good for a marina's image to have a burned out hulk at the docks?"

"The Coast Guard says it's an environmental hazard waiting to happen," she said. "It's still floating normally, though. The only water in her is from the fire hoses."

"Phantom Services will be back soon," I told her. "Assuming we accept their estimate."

"We should both stay here until that job is done," she said. "Let the insurance company take care of the mess in Fort Myers Beach."

I called Fred and filled him in. He wasn't terribly upset. It was only money.

"Once you're seen back at this marina," I told him. "You might consider quietly relocating far away from here."

"You're probably right," he said. "But I hate to give those assholes the satisfaction."

"They can't bother you if they don't know where you are," I said. "You could take this thing to the south of France if you wanted to."

"I'll give it some thought," he said. "Thanks."

Eight

No bad actors made a move against the new Hatteras. The installation of the security system went smoothly. When it was finished, Brody and I learned how to use it. It was quite simple actually. All the feeds came to our phones or any other device we chose. You could see all the cameras, zoom them in, and swivel them to look around the boat. Motion detectors alerted you of any intruders larger than a seagull. The system also monitored cabin temperatures and water levels in the bilge compartments. It could be armed or disarmed with the touch of a finger. If there were a serious breach, alarms sounded and the nearest law enforcement was automatically notified. Short of a missile attack, the boat was safe.

Fred flew in so we could be done with the project and return to our lives. He was thrilled with the new boat and the security system.

"I knew I could count on you two," he said. "What's my bill for your services?"

"Whatever you think is fair," I said. "It wasn't exactly hard work."

"A nice vacation for you," he said. "Maybe you should be paying me. You still holding onto the last hunk of change I paid you?"

"Haven't touched it," I said. "We're doing all right on what we already had."

"Good news," he said. "It's clear Brody is a good influence on you. You're starting to act and look less like a bum."

"I think that may be a compliment," I said.

"I'll wire another hundred grand to the same account," he said. "I really do appreciate you helping me out. You've got plenty to get this gal her new boat."

"I'd just like to get back to my old boat for now," I said. "We've been gone a lot lately."

Before we left I took Fred up in the pilothouse and went over the controls with him.

I explained how she responded and gave him my best advice.

"Maybe I should just call you whenever I want to go someplace," he said, laughing.

"You'll get the hang of it in no time," I said. "It really handles nicely."

"I better," he said. "A man can't have some bum drive his boat better than he can."

"Looks like I'll be learning to drive my own new boat before long," I offered.

"I sense your reluctance, son," he said. "But you can't expect a woman like Brody to live on your old tub forever. You're in a position these days to pamper her if that's what she wants."

"We do seem to have lost our wanderlust," I admitted. "We seem fine with sitting in the marina."

"Do it in style and comfort then," he said. "Treat yourself to the finer things for a change."

I was under pressure from the two people I cared about the most. I was being nudged and cajoled to do something that I really didn't want to do. The points they both made were completely valid. I was on the losing side of the argument. Still, deep inside, I resented being forced. I didn't like being told what to do, even if it was the right thing. I struggled to come to terms with the situation. How could I stay true to myself and still make everyone else happy? I didn't have the answer, other than to suck it up and play along. I'd never been very good at that strategy.

We made our way back to the marina and *Leap of Faith*. When we walked inside, I caught a vague whiff of poop. We opened her up and aired her out. The smell went away. Brody flushed the head and the smell returned. I'd never had an odor problem before. I got a flashlight and investigated. The holding tank wasn't leaking. The hoses and fittings all seemed fine. I thought the odor was because she'd been sitting unused for so long.

Over the next two days, we again noticed the smell every time one of us flushed. I got the holding tank pumped out and overdosed it with deodorizer. The problem persisted. Finally, I'd had enough. We moved furniture to get at the floor hatches. As soon as I opened the forward compartment I saw the source of the smell. The vacuum generator for our Vacu-flush head had exploded in a geyser of goo. The device was covered in shit. It had run down into the bilge as well. Other than burning down or sinking, I couldn't think of a worse problem for a boat to have. It was disgusting.

I went outside to get some air. I told Brody not to look. In fact, I told her to leave for a few hours at least. I instructed her not to use the head again until it was fixed. She grabbed her pool bag and a towel and disappeared, holding her nose on the way out. I sat and thought about how to proceed. I couldn't wait. I had to attack the problem right then. After working up the nerve and breathing deep of clean air, I got to work.

I brought the garden hose right into the cabin. The docks there had very high water pressure. I blasted the entire apparatus and surrounding area with a hard stream of water until it was relatively clean. The bilge wasn't clean though. A murky mixture of sewage and water ran towards the main pump. I shut it off so as not to pump the filth overboard. What to do with it? I used a shop vac to fill a five-gallon bucket. I carried the bucket off the boat and dumped it in an inconspicuous spot. Don't ask me where. I repeated the process over and over again. When the bilge was mostly dry, I squirted a bleach and water mix all over the place. I left it to soak.

I got my tools and a light and climbed down into a narrow space between the battery bank and the vacuum generator. It was the only place down there that didn't have any room to work. I had no choice but to remove the whole thing and work on it outside. I twisted and contorted myself until the hoses and power cables were disconnected. I hauled the foul-smelling contraption up out of the bilge and carried it to the back deck. I ran clean water through it and over it for a good twenty minutes. I disassembled it and inspected all its components. It used a bellows to force product from the head to the holding tank by creating a vacuum. The bellows were badly torn. I needed to order the part. There was no way to repair it.

I cleaned up the work area and I cleaned up myself. After a long shower, I explained to Brody what we needed. She found the part on Amazon and had it shipped to the marina. We used the marina facilities for the next two days while waiting for the part to come in. It was a satisfactory arrangement except for those middle of the night emergencies. I figured no one was watching at three in the morning so I peed over the side. Brody used a bucket. Sometimes you just have to do what you have to do.

The next day I again used the shop vac to clean up the bleach mixture I'd sprayed. I'd managed to clean up almost every inch of the affected area, except for the piece of plywood the vacuum generator sat on. It was simply saturated with liquid poop. It fell apart as I attempted to remove it. I gathered all the sewage soaked pieces and bagged them. It was disgusting. After another round of cleanup, I drove to Home Depot for a new piece of plywood. I glued the newly custom cut section to the stringers with 5200 Marine Sealant.

When the part finally arrived I fumbled with installing it. I had it put back together and reinstalled but it didn't work. It also made a loud clacking noise. I'd screwed up something. I took it back out again and puzzled over it. I disassembled and reassembled the damn thing three times before I got it right. I screwed it down to the plywood, attached the hoses, and hooked up the wires.

"Flush Brody," I said.

"You sure?" she asked.

It worked. No poop spewed from the top of it. I checked all the connections again before asking for another flush. It stayed together and worked as it was supposed to.

I showered yet again and thought to myself. *Fuck a boat. I'm buying a cabin in the woods.*

That thought smacked me upside the head like a sledgehammer. A few other thoughts rattled loose and fell out along with it. The litany of drama that had dominated my life over the past seven years was a direct result of my boating lifestyle. The underside of living as a boat bum was the cause of my conflicts. The crazy characters, the drugs, and the damsels in distress were all the result of living on the fringes of society. As much as I'd attempted to avoid trouble, it had always found me. At first, I'd had no choice but to continue living on a boat. I couldn't afford to do anything else. Now, I had money. I didn't need to keep doing it. I had options. Why it had never occurred to me before, I'm not sure. Brody hadn't brought it up. How would she react?

The last piece of the puzzle was *Miss Leap*. Trading her for a nicer boat would be like stabbing her in the back. Moving to a cabin in the woods would be much less of a betrayal. She'd understand. I warmed to the idea. I thought it might be nice to hide out in a cozy little cabin off the beaten path, away from life's ills. I pictured myself hauling wood and sitting by a roaring fire. I thought about the cold and the snow. In the past, I'd hated snow because I had to go to work in it. It made life difficult. I hadn't worked in years and didn't need to. Let it snow. I'd throw another log on the fire and ride it out.

The more I thought about it, the more I liked it. I got dressed and went to find Brody. I couldn't wait to see her reaction.

"What do you think about a cabin in the woods? I asked her.

"What?" she asked. "Where did this come from?"

"This particular epiphany was a product of poop in the bilge," I said. "But I'm serious. Let's think about it."

"I never thought you'd be willing to leave the water," she said. "Or this boat."

"The only thing constant in life is change," I told her. "I think it's time to move on. Start anew."

"A cabin does seem romantic," she said. "How do you feel about the mountains?"

"You'd seriously consider it?" I asked.

"Sure would," she said. "I just didn't ever want to question living aboard. Like I said, I never thought you'd consider moving to land."

"I'm considering it now," I said. "I just need your full enthusiastic approval. Be honest with me."

"Breeze, I'd love to have a house," she began. "I'd like a bathtub. I'd like to brush my teeth in the bathroom and not at the galley sink. I'd like for the roof to not leak when it rains. I'd like a big old bed that I can stretch out in. I'd like a little garden. I'd like to see humming-birds and deer. I'd like to flush the damn toilet paper for a change."

"Okay but not in some suburban neighbor-hood," I said. "I'm talking about privacy and peace. No neighbors."

"As long as it's a reasonable drive to town," she said. "You're serious aren't you?"

"If you say yes, we'll make it happen," I said.

"I'll be damned," she said. "I can't remember being this shocked, but I'm totally onboard."

"How do we go about finding what we want?" I asked.

"The internet, silly," she said. "I'll drag you into the future yet."

We spent the next week diligently working on two objectives: preparing the boat to show to prospective buyers and searching for the perfect cabin. On the boat front, I realized that I'd neglected several maintenance items. I'd been too busy doing nothing except floating in the pool or sitting in the air conditioning. Summer had arrived, and the heat was getting to me. During all those years living in Florida with no air conditioning, it hadn't bothered me. Now that we had cool air, the heat just clobbered me. Brody suggested that the blood pressure medication may have something to do with it as well. Nevertheless, I set about toiling in the summer sun. I wanted to turn *Miss Leap* over to her new owners in fine shape. It was a matter of pride. She'd been so good to me, I had to be good to her.

Brody worked inside, going through our meager belongings and cleaning like a madwoman. In the evening we scoured the web for log cabins. We decided to limit our search to a few states. We included Kentucky, Tennessee, Georgia and the Carolinas. My blood was too thin to consider moving to Maine or Alaska, even though that's where the best deals were. We signed up for a few subscription services that sent us emails every day with more cabins to consider. I would have been fine with an off-grid shack, but Brody needed some amenities and the ability to go to town whenever she felt like it. She wanted a bathtub. We both wanted a fireplace or wood burning stove. The place needed a nice covered porch to sit and watch the wildlife. We also had a budget for this purchase. We had plenty of money, but we couldn't blow it all on a fancy chalet. It would have to last us a very long time. We'd also need to furnish the place, which I assumed would be expensive.

The search went on for another few weeks until we hit on something with the potential to meet all of our wants. It was near Banner Elk, North Carolina, high on a mountain overlooking Valle Crucis. It had two bedrooms and a loft. It also had two bathrooms and a big old Whirlpool tub. A Franklin stove sat on a stone hearth in the open living area. The back porch looked perfect. The ad boasted of a babbling brook running through the property. We continued looking at other houses but kept coming back to this one. We sent an email. The guy asked me to give him a call.

His name was Richard and he was a log home builder. His company was called Eagle Ridge, after the hillside where the cabin sat. There were a few other cabins on that mountain, but he assured me the one we had found was very quiet and private. I arranged to go take a look at it in person.

"Looks like we're driving to North Carolina," I told Brody.

"Now?"

"Tuesday. We meet him at one o'clock," I said. "We'll get a room somewhere the night before."

"Road trip and a hotel," she said. "Sounds like fun."

We headed north early Monday morning. I took I-75 beyond Tampa, then exited onto 301 near Ocala. We stayed on 301 all the way to I-95 just south of the Georgia line. It was the same route we'd taken while running from Hurricane Irma. The sights were familiar. The ride was much more relaxing this time. We stopped in Columbia and checked into a Hampton Inn just in time for dinner. I noticed a renewed twinkle in Brody's eyes during dinner.

"No offense to *Leap of Faith*," she said. "But I'm excited about this."

"Let's not get ahead of ourselves," I said. "We haven't even laid eyes on the place yet."

"It's going to work out," she assured me.

"Shit always works out," I said, smiling.

The next day it rained heavily the entire trip. We crept up a mountainside near Boone with near zero visibility. Fog rolled in. We got behind a tractor-trailer doing twenty miles per hour. I followed his flashing emergency lights as we drove through switchback after switchback. Brody's ears popped as we gained elevation. The deluge eased a bit as we turned onto the last mountain road. It had even more twists and turns than the previous one. Up we went until the road leveled off at four thousand feet. There sat the cabin, on a small semi-flat spot at the top of the ridge.

We parked in front of it right on time. I texted Richard and he arrived in minutes. The three of us went inside to take a look. It wasn't perfect, but it felt right. It was a bit on the rustic side, which I liked. The downstairs living area was open to the kitchen. The loft ran the entire length of the cabin. Small dormer windows let in light at either end. I breathed in the smell of wood and was inspired. I pictured a writing desk in front of one of those windows. I could sit up there for hours writing down my stories. I certainly had enough experiences to fill the pages of a book or two. It was a nice quiet place to think.

The master bedroom was large enough for a king bed, which made Brody happy. It also had its own separate full bath. The place was luxurious compared to living on a boat. We went out on the back porch and listened to the brook gurgle over the moss covered rocks.

"We can put in a fire pit right there," said Brody. "Sit out here on cool autumn nights and drink hot chocolate by the fire."

"I like the sound of that stream," I said. "It's comforting."

From the backyard, we looked around at the scenery. The trees were in full greenery.

"You say there are more cabins up here?" I asked Richard.

"You can't see them in the summertime," he said. "Once the leaves are gone you can make out a few of them."

"Nice people?"

"They are here for the same reasons you are," he said. "Peace, quiet and privacy.

"My kind of neighbors," I said.

Brody and I looked at each other and communicated silently. I could tell by her eyes that she approved of the place. We gave each other a nod.

"Okay Richard," I said. "Let's make some kind of deal."

While hashing out the particulars, Richard asked me what I did for a living. I paused for a few seconds before figuring out something to say.

"High-end odd jobs," I said. "My last gig was to install sophisticated surveillance equipment on a hundred foot yacht."

"So you're in security?"

"Not always," I explained. "Search and salvage, treasure hunting, boat delivery, all of it nautical."

"Not much call for that kind of work in the mountains," he said.

"I'm taking an early retirement," I said. "Our finances are secure as long as we don't get carried away."

"Speaking of finances," he said. "Have you talked to mortgage lenders?"

"We'll be paying cash," I said.

That got his eyebrows up.

Nine

I should have learned my lesson after we bought a new car with cash. Normal people don't just walk into a dealership and plop down cash for their purchase. It makes salesmen suspicious. It irritates the finance guy. It takes money away from the dealership because they can't sell you a loan. They wonder if you're a drug dealer. Richard wouldn't benefit if I got a bank loan though. It shouldn't make any difference to him. He recovered from his initial shock quickly.

"Cash is okay," he said. "I like cash."

Maybe he could hide that income from the taxman. I didn't care if he did.

Eventually, we worked out an arrangement. There was some additional paperwork required and the settlement couldn't happen immediately. I also needed more time to get the boat ready for sale. The end result was a move-in date scheduled for the first of August. We shook hands and drove back down the mountain. We took a brief tour of Banner Elk on the way home. It had one stoplight and a short stretch of road with various business establishments. Fine dining places dotted the hillside on either side of the road. There was one grocery store and a Lowes. Signs advertised the various ski resorts nearby.

It was a world away from southwest Florida.

The rain started up again and we drove in silence. The only voice was Brody's phone telling me which road to take next. When we reached the interstate, Brody spoke up.

"I feel like I'm in a state of shock," she said. "This is all happening so fast. Now I'm thinking about all the things we'll be leaving behind. All the memories."

"Me too," I admitted. "We couldn't be making a more drastic change. From the beach to the mountains."

"At the same time, it's exciting," she said. "A whole new beginning."

"It will be good for us," I said. "Let's just hope we can stand the winters."

"Get me an electric blanket and keep the fire going," she said.

"Body heat will become our friend instead of our enemy," I suggested.

"Good point," she said. "I guess this is really happening."

"We can change our minds," I said. "We've both got to be committed to this."

"No," she said. "Let's do this. Let's learn to love the mountains as much as we loved the beach."

"I'm willing," I said.

"Then it's final," she said.

"Done deal."

It continued to rain all the way back to Florida. As we crossed the state line, it was coming down so hard we were crawling along the I-95 at thirty miles per hour. I made a snap decision and took the exit for Fernandina Beach. We found a room for the night. We ate at an oceanside restaurant. After our meal, the rain stopped. We walked out on the beach and watched the waves roll in. We combed the sand looking for treasures like we'd done so many times on so many beaches. The rain returned and chased us back to the hotel. That moment had a ring of finality to it like we'd just walked our last beach. We felt just a little bit sad.

A six-pack and a bottle of rum cured the blues. A nice hot shower washed away the melancholy. It was time to look forward. A new life awaited. We made it the rest of the way back the next day and got to work on *Miss Leap*.

We listed the boat on a website called Boat Trader. It got us a few nibbles but nothing serious. Craigslist provided no leads at all. Eventually, we decided to sign up with a broker. If it hadn't sold before we left, we'd leave it in the water and let the broker show it to prospective buyers.

We rented storage space and started removing stuff from the boat. Where did all the stuff come from? This process raised the waterline several inches. We went furniture shopping. It was surreal to look at sofas and bedroom sets.

It was downright foreign, but we kept our eyes on the prize. We'd rent a truck and arrive with at least enough furniture to get us by until we could get more. Brody occupied herself by shopping for rugs, lamps, and decorations. She was enjoying the prospect of becoming a home owning domestic.

As the time passed, we became disillusioned with the boat life. All of a sudden we were just done with it. The decision had been made. We felt like we were just killing time until our cabin life began. The Florida sun got hotter. The afternoon thunderstorms got more severe. Red tide caused a massive fish kill on our favorite beaches. Political discord and civil strife got out of hand. We couldn't wait to disappear into the mountains of North Carolina. Both of us had several skin cancers removed. We stopped sunning by the pool. The old air conditioner was no longer doing its job. We replaced it and spent more and more time staying inside the cool cabin. There was no doubt that our life in Florida was over. We had another month to wait. Our impatience grew.

Then we got a phone call from Captain Fred. We jumped at the opportunity to do anything other than sitting inside *Leap of Faith*.

"Some shady looking characters have been eyeballing my boat," said Fred. "They haven't tried anything yet, but I keep seeing the same two guys hanging out in the marina. They're too interested in my boat to ignore."

"What do you need us to do?" I asked.

"If we run them off they'll just send someone else," he said. "Whoever it is, they're probably waiting for me to arrive to verify that it's mine."

"If we do nothing they might find the opportunity to torch it like they did *Incognito*."

"I hate to intrude on your life of leisure," he said. "But can you take her out of there? Just go someplace where they won't find you until I can figure out where to go next."

"We'd be happy to," I said. "But we'll need to be back within a month."

"What? You got an appointment with your parole officer?" he asked jokingly.

"Just something we need to do," I said.

"Give me a few weeks," he said. "You don't even need to report in. I can track your every movement. I'll catch up with you."

A joyride vacation on a luxury yacht wasn't a bad way to waste some time. It could be our last hurrah. Fred's accommodations were better than a fine hotel. At the same time, there might be some danger involved. Who was after Fred now? What did they want? How far would they go to extract their revenge? Brody and I had to snap out of our funk and get serious about our personal safety. We needed to recall those sharp senses that had become dull. Our cabin in the woods would have to wait. We had one last mission before we left Florida.

Brody and I sat down with her computer. We pulled up Fred's marina and studied the layout. We decided to see if we could identify the strange men before we boarded his boat. We would both carry weapons. We got Fred to send us photos of the suspects. While we discussed possible locations for hiding out, I was hit with yet another epiphany.

"Why not turn this into another relief mission?" I asked.

"While I admire your generosity, I was more looking forward to a relaxing getaway," said Brody.

"This will be our last chance," I said. "We won't have a boat, or access to anything like Fred's boat once we leave for good."

"Who do we help?" she asked.

"Good question," I answered. "I guess the first step is to see who still needs it."

I left that research up to Brody. I studied the faces of the two men at the marina. They were average looking Floridians, chosen to blend in. They weren't hard men. They were probably just scouts who'd report back to someone who could send hard men later. I saw no sign of concealed weapons. Maybe the best tactic would be to climb aboard and promptly vacate the premises. They'd have no idea where we were headed. I didn't even know where we'd be headed yet.

Brody decided that St. Croix was one of the islands that still needed aid. St. John and St. Thomas had gotten all the early resources directed to the U.S. Virgin Islands. The people's needs were similar to those in Puerto Rico. The governor down there was actively working with FEMA and directing donations to The Community Foundation of the V.I. He asked those that wanted to organize missions to bring food, water, cots and personal hygiene items. We could carry tons of that stuff on Fred's boat.

We stopped our planning efforts to have a beer.

"To Benevolent Breeze," said Brody, raising her bottle. "A man always on a mission."

"And his faithful sidekick, Brody," I said. "Cheers."

The die was cast. We would sneak Fred's yacht out of Fort Myers and load it up with relief supplies for St. Croix. We'd keep it away from prying eyes and hang out in an island paradise. I couldn't think of a more fitting end to my nautical journeys. It would put the final punctuation mark on an epic episode in my life.

We still had to work out the logistics of the combined missions. We couldn't load the boat in Fort Myers. We needed to roll out of there fast and load up quickly someplace else. We wouldn't have a car, making things more challenging. Brody searched for a marina south of Fort Myers that could handle a hundred foot boat. Naples was the only logical choice. I called the Naples Boat Club to see if they had a spot for us. They assured me that they did. Brody shifted her efforts to the delivery of goods to our vessel. I don't know why we didn't think of it the first time, but in this modern age, you can have anything delivered right to your door in a matter of days.

Fred called with more news. He had spotted a third man in the marina.

"I wouldn't have connected him at first," he said. "But he spoke with both the other guys. Rough looking fellow."

The picture he sent depicted the kind of hard man I'd been worried about. He had a square chin with a three-day stubble. His brow protruded almost like that of a caveman. He had hands like hammers. His nose had been busted a few times. He was compact and powerful looking. He clearly wasn't the brains of the operation. He was the muscle. Why was he there?

"What the hell is going on, Fred?" I asked. "It's almost like they know we're about to make a move."

"I doubt they've been able to intercept my communications," he said. "Must be on your end."

"You think they can listen to Brody's phone?"

"I can think of no other explanation," he said. "Toss that phone and get back to me on a new line."

I was being pulled back in. Brody and I both were being sucked into something that we'd hoped to avoid. Managing surveillance of Brody's phone was not the work of amateurs. We had no reason to believe the government was involved. Someone with a sophisticated level of technology was after Fred but was using us to get to him. I regretted allowing Brody to ever reacquire her devices. We thought the heat was off permanently.

"Trash that phone and all your computer shit," I told Brody. "We'll go get a burner like we did before."

"Sorry, Breeze," she said. "I had no idea that someone would go that far."

"Me neither," I said. "But technology is going to be the death of us all. Somewhere, someday, someone can get access to all your data if they want it."

"Tough to live without it these days," she said. "We just searched for marinas and delivery services five minutes ago."

"I'll admit it makes life easier," I said. "But for now we need to do without."

She cut up the SIM card while I smashed the phone and tossed it overboard. We purchased a cheap disposable phone and pre-paid for thirty minutes with cash. I called Fred while we were still away from the boat. Maybe they had me bugged, who knows?

"How much time are these guys spending at the marina?" I asked.

"They come and go most of the daylight hours," he said. "Don't see them after dark."

"Doesn't mean they aren't close by," I said. "Could be sitting in the parking lot watching who comes and goes."

"Could be," he said. "If that's the case, how are you going to get in without being seen?"

"I'll figure something out," I said. "No way that I want to confront that caveman."

"You be careful, son," he said.

Brody was none too pleased about this latest development.

"What have you gotten us into now?" she asked. "We were this close to leaving this kind of shit behind forever."

"Blame Captain Fred," I offered.

"You could have just said no," she countered.

"No, I couldn't," I explained. "The money he's paid us is making our new life possible. I can't turn him down on this. It will be the last time. I promise."

"How many one-more-times have there been already?" she asked. "It's got to end with this."

"You're right," I said. "This will end it."

We started working on a plan to gain access to Fred's boat without being stopped. We considered going in disguised as boat detailers. We'd spend the afternoon scrubbing and polishing. When the men left we'd take off. Then we realized that they probably knew what we looked like. If they had tapped into our phone, they certainly had a picture of us. We ruled out any attempt from land. We'd have to come by water. I wished I could pull up the marina's website and take another look at the layout, but we'd destroyed Brody's tablet.

We went to the nearest library. They wouldn't let us use the computers without first getting a library card. We had to prove we were residents of the county. We couldn't do that. I had no knowledge of anything resembling an internet café in the area. We had no way to search for one. We ended up in Port Charlotte at the local Best Buy. Brody browsed the different tablets and asked the clerk some questions. We didn't need a nine-hundred dollar iPad, just something that could access the internet. She settled on a Kindle Fire. If you did not register the device with any of your previous accounts, it wouldn't show who you were. It also lacked a

GPS, making it harder to track. We bought it and went to the nearest McDonald's for free Wi-Fi.

Fort Myer's Yacht Basin was in the downtown historic district, right between the two Route 41 bridges. Centennial Park was at the foot of the Cleveland Avenue Bridge, just five blocks from the marina. It looked like a good place to launch a kayak. There were several places to find long-term parking within a few blocks of the park. There was only one main dock to gain access to the boat slips. Anyone sitting in the parking lot could easily spot new arrivals, but they wouldn't be able to see a kayak in the water, especially in the dark at three a.m. I hoped that the noise from the bridge would drown out the engine noise when I fired up Fred's boat. If not, we'd have to clear out of the slip very quickly. I had the information that I needed.

We went back to the marina. Kayaks and paddleboards were sold on site. We picked out a dark green double seater. We tried to put together dark clothing to wear. We each had black shorts but needed a long sleeve black shirt. That turned out to be hard to find in Florida. We ended up at a Goodwill store where we purchased button-down black shirts for a few bucks. We had to settle for black ball caps, as there are no ski masks to be found in the entire state.

We filled our backpacks with a few essentials. We strapped the kayak to the roof of the car and waited for the right time.

"I don't have to remind you to be on your toes," I told Brody. "Time to turn on those G-man instincts."

"I'm ready," she said. "But I'll be glad when it's over."

"If we get in and out fast it will just be a boat ride," I said. "But if there's trouble that caveman worries me."

"So we shoot instead of fight," she said.

"Which will rain down hell on our heads," I said. "We need to avoid him at all costs."

I'd beaten a man much stronger than me once. He was a big Russian with a seriously thick skull. A sharp rap to the head with a cue ball barely fazed him. A steel pipe to the head stopped him briefly, long enough for me to break his knee with a swift side kick. If I were any judge he was a softie compared to the caveman. He had the look of someone unafraid of violence, accustomed to it. I shuddered at the thought of him getting his hands on me.

Brody and I hadn't spent much time talking about the time we both shot a man to death. It was the second time for her. My first shooting but also the second time causing another man's death. It was a weird thing for a couple to have in common. We'd simply put it behind us and moved on. We both understood the gravity of what we'd done. For each of us, the first time was under questionable circumstances. We couldn't go back and fix that. The second time was self-defense. We were completely justified, but that didn't make it much easier. I quizzed Brody on her state of mind.

"I apologize for putting us in a situation where violence might become necessary," I began. "How's your head on this?"

"If I'm in the game, I'm in it to win," she said. "I'll do whatever is necessary."

"I don't question that," I said. "I just want to be clear about what could go down. Neither one of us can let the past affect our decisions here. We need to react with decisive speed. We can philosophize about it later, as long as we survive."

"Understood," she said. "I'm clear in the head. I haven't lost my nerve."

She had every right to question my state of mind, but she did not. She had focused her concentration on the task at hand. I did the same. We left for Fort Myers at two in the morning. The park was deserted when we arrived. We unloaded the kayak on the wet grass near the shore. Brody stayed with it while I found a parking spot for the car. There were a few cars crossing the bridges, but the surface streets were empty.

We slid the kayak in the water, got our balance, and began paddling towards the yacht basin. We didn't need to be quiet yet, but we kept our voices to a whisper. We worked on smooth splash-free strokes with our paddles. The five blocks went by too quickly. The job was upon us before we knew it. We snuck silently along the docks until we came alongside Fred's boat. There was no sign of life in the marina. We had worked out our individual duties beforehand so there was no need to speak.

We crept aboard and went straight for the dock lines. I freed the aft lines while Brody went to the bow. I scrambled to the bridge and waited for her signal. As soon as she untied the last line she gave me a thumbs up. I fired both engines. Their roar broke the silence of the night. Even at the lowest throttle setting, they sounded like a locomotive. I shifted into forward. The caveman appeared on the dock. Brody stared at him through the sights of her gun. As we cleared the last piling I throttled up hard. Once again, I was leaving a fancy marina in the middle of the night while throwing a huge wake at the other vessels. If I kept this up, Captain Fred wouldn't be welcome anywhere. I looked back to see the caveman staring back at us. He didn't raise a weapon or hurl obscenities. He stood there like a stone, his clenched fists at his side.

We went out into the Caloosahatchee and headed for the Gulf of Mexico. Brody joined me on the bridge.

"Dude's even scarier in person," she said. "Makes a big target though."

"I'm just glad he was a few seconds too slow," I said.

"So I can relax now?"

"He can't get to us out here," I told her. "Why don't you go below and get some rest?"

"I'm too wound up to sleep," she said. "You go ahead. I'll wake you before we get to Naples."

"Take us out into the Gulf," I said. "We've got to kill some time before the marina opens."

I was not wound up like Brody. The adrenaline was gone and I was tired. Before I drifted off to sleep something started nagging me. I'd overlooked something but I couldn't put my finger on it. Before I could determine what it was, I passed out. The caveman came to me in my sleep. In my dream, he was twice as big and had the fangs of a saber-toothed tiger. It terrified me so much that it startled me awake. I sat up in bed and looked around the stateroom. As soon as I figured out where I was, the nagging feeling returned. I shook off the nightmare and turned on the coffee-maker.

It came to me after the first cup. If our unknown adversary had monitored our communications, they would know we were headed to Naples. The caveman would be waiting at the marina for our arrival. I don't think my fear of him was exaggerated. Something told me that he wanted to break my bones. I didn't want to ever have to shoot another man, but if he cornered me, I'd have no choice.

Ten

The sun was just coming up as I joined Brody on the bridge. I let the moment happen before telling her about my suspicion.

"That's just frigging great," she said. "Do we have enough fuel to get to the Keys?"

"I was wondering how we're going to take on supplies for St. Croix," I said.

"Our plan has gone to shit," she said. "Maybe we should rethink this whole thing."

"Adapt and overcome," I said. "We can still pull this off."

"We can't even make a phone call out here," she said. "We're flying blind."

I made a quick mental calculation on the fuel situation. We'd be fine. I set a course for the Seven Mile Bridge. Even though we couldn't get a big enough slip in Marathon, we could still take on fuel there. I tried to remain positive about our situation. At least we'd made a clean escape from Fort Myers. The caveman hadn't taken our heads off either. That was a real plus. It was a nice day to be on the Gulf in a luxury yacht. Out of sight of land, the water turned blue. The sea was calm and the sun was shining. I'd certainly been through worse times.

I was going to miss all of that. I'd melded my life with the ways of the sea. I'd become one with it. I'd grown to love southwest Florida with her white sand beaches and warm weather. All of my excursions to the islands had broadened my appreciation of the tropical life. Someday soon I'd be shoveling snow, wearing layers of clothing to ward off the cold. Could I make the transition? It had its pros and cons. Here on the water, I'd never been truly isolated from people. Boats came and went like the tides. I'd made friends in various ports. I'd loved my share of women. Up in the mountains, we'd be alone, but we'd be alone together, even if it became a wintry wonderland. We could shed the distractions and concentrate on each other. We could sleep together in a big bed without sharing our sweat or swatting mosquitoes. We'd have room to stretch and fresh mountain air to breathe.

A field of stone crab traps snapped me back to reality. I maneuvered through the minefield and diverted my attention to our mission. Where could we load the boat with the necessary goods? I used the GPS to look ahead. There was no good place in the Keys. The closest Walmart was in Homestead. I inched the screen further north to Biscayne Bay. I knew that Key Biscayne couldn't accommodate us. Next was Miami. I hated Miami. I really didn't want to deal with that. I sat there staring at the map until my eyes landed on Dinner Key. It was directly across the bay from Key Biscayne. I was certain we could acquire everything we needed there.

"Here," I said to Brody, pointing at the map. "Dinner Key. We'll take the outside route from Boot Key up to the entrance to Biscayne Bay."

"It'd be nice to know what's nearby," she said.

"I have an idea about that," I said. "This thing is tricked out with sophisticated electronics that operate off satellites. Fred can get a live feed from anywhere in the world. Surely it can connect us to the internet."

"Probably has a router for Wi-Fi coverage throughout the boat," she said. "Most likely password protected."

"Go get your Kindle," I said. "Look for a signal."

It was there. It was labeled *Incognito*. It required a password.

"Have you seen a Sat phone laying around anywhere?" I asked Brody.

"I wasn't looking for one, but no," she answered. "I'll go look around." She came back empty-handed.

"Looks like you can make calls right through the ship's systems, via the computer," she said. "But it's password protected too."

"Why can't we just email Fred?" I asked. "Ask him for the passwords."

"I didn't set up my email account so this stupid tablet wouldn't know who I am," she said.

"Just make up a new one," I said. "Give it false information."

"Why didn't I think of that?" she said. "I'm supposed to be the tech savvy one."

"If it comes right down to it, the marina will have Wi-Fi," I said. "We'll hail them on the radio to get a slip. It will only add another day or so to arrange deliveries. I would like to investigate the marina situation in St. Croix though. I looked at a few of them but I don't remember the particulars. We'll also have to get in touch with that Community Association."

"You see," said Brody. "These modern gadgets come in handy."

"If we could only stop them from spying on us," I countered.

I spent some time playing around with the electronics on the helm. It was past time to figure out just what their capabilities were. I had started to worry that the vessel's deep draft and wide beam might be a problem entering Boot Key. I wanted to check out Faro Blanco on the Ocean Side. It would be more convenient.

The big chart plotter was a touchscreen model. I poked around the screen until I found the satellite view. I zoomed in on Faro Blanco Resort and Marina. It was a neat machine, but it showed me a tight space with very narrow fairways. The fuel dock didn't appear capable of handling a hundred foot vessel. I moved the screen back over to Boot Key. I switched back and forth from chart mode to satellite mode. It could be done. I'd just have to be careful. I'd also need high tide.

We cruised along at mid-speed on our way south. I mindlessly stared out over the water but stayed alert for crab and lobster traps. Something crept into my thoughts. My gut was telling me that I'd missed something else somewhere along the way. I'll be damned if I could figure out what it was. Either I was getting too old for this type of work, or I was too far out of practice. It bothered me to think I was losing my edge. On the other hand, I had remembered that the caveman might know we were headed to Naples. It had avoided me at first, but I realized it in time to avoid disaster. I gave myself credit for that much. Whatever it was, it would come to me sooner or later.

We wouldn't make it in time. The fuel docks would be closed. We'd have to anchor for the night. I checked the switches for the windlass. They had no power. I went to the breaker box and flipped the windlass switch. I went forward to inspect the anchor. It was a huge stainless affair. There were foot switches on the bow and a rocker switch at the helm to control the windlass. I gave them each a bump in both directions to make sure they worked.

We passed under the Seven Mile Bridge in the early evening. I approached Boot Key and eased back on the throttles. I took us as shallow as I dared and dropped the hook. Once we settled back on the chain, I put it in reverse and throttled up. The anchor dug in quickly and held us firm. We were good for the night. It was time for an anchor-down beer. The best thing about the anchorage was its view of the sunset. I intended to be pleasantly buzzed when it happened.

Brody joined me on the aft deck. We were free of bugs offshore. The evening was pleasant. The beers went down smoothly.

"Aren't you going to miss this?" Brody asked.

"Of course I will," I admitted. "The key is to not look back. No regrets."

"I don't know," she said. "Sometimes it's nice to look back on fond memories."

"Agreed, but we don't live in the past," I said. "I spent a lifetime on the Chesapeake. I spent many, many days on a boat somewhere in her waters. I thought I'd miss it, but I didn't. Florida was so much better. I made it my new home and never looked back."

"We'll make North Carolina our new home," she said.

"If it doesn't suit us, we can always pack up and go somewhere else," I said.

"It's funny," she said. "People just don't think like that."

"They don't have the freedom that we do," I said. "They've got a job and kids in school. They've got roots that are tough to pull up."

"Soccer practice. Older parents to take care of. Community ties."

"All that stuff," I said. "I'm not faulting them, but packing up for someplace new just isn't feasible. We're the lucky ones."

"Didn't you ever just want to settle down and raise a family like normal folks?"

"I did that," I said. "Just like everyone else. I was happy too, until it all got ripped away. I can't ever go back to that. Is that what you want?"

"Not now," she said. "I dreamed about it when I was younger. Then I learned how screwed up the world is. I'm sort of glad I never had kids. I moved around with the Bureau and never put down roots."

"Let's see how this North Carolina thing works out," I said. "Maybe that can become home for us."

"I'm still looking forward to it," she said.

"Me too."

We brought out some snacks and a bottle of rum. The sun put on a spectacular show for us. Once it got dark we buttoned up the ship. I armed all of the fancy security stuff that I had helped install. I checked on the next day's tides. Brody advised me to put down my work and come to bed before she fell asleep. I took her advice and I was glad I did.

I slept soundly. No cavemen came to visit me in my dreams. I don't recall dreaming at all, except for that nagging feeling that I'd missed some crucial detail. I dismissed it and enjoyed my unconsciousness.

We had time for breakfast before the tide was right to enter Boot Key Harbor. I tended to bacon while Brody flipped pancakes. We stood elbow to elbow at the fanciest range I'd ever seen on a boat.

"This is pretty damn nice," she said. "I could live with a galley like this."

"We will never be able to afford a boat like this," I told her. "Unless you want me to work a ton of missions. I'm sure Captain Fred can hook me up."

"Scratch that," she said. "I'll have to settle for our little country kitchen."

"I'm sure you'll make it your own in no time," I said.

"You ain't seen nothing yet, Breezy Boy," she said. "I'll put twenty pounds on you the first month."

"I'll have to cut back on the booze to keep my girlish figure."

"Or switch to bourbon," she said. "Rum's got all that sugar in it."

"Now that's the kind of creative thinking that I can appreciate," I said.

The tide came in and we pulled up the anchor. We crawled painfully slow into the channel. I called out on channel 16 for any other vessel that might be transiting the narrow strip of water. I needed all of it. Fishing boats gave way and allowed me enough room to squeeze my way up to Pancho's Fuel Dock. The attendants seemed excited to see such a large boat at their dock. They were further astounded by the fuel bill when they finished. I saved the receipt for Fred and tipped generously.

Upon leaving Pancho's, I had to continue inward past Burdine's. I nosed into the blank space between the restaurant and the abandoned marina to the east. I backed out into the channel once again to reverse course. I worked the controls gingerly, making small bursts from the engines in order to control our movement. I called over the radio again to announce our departure. The exit cleared and we left the harbor. We motored out beyond Sombrero Reef and turned toward Biscayne Bay.

Fred's yacht was a joy to pilot. The ultra-modern controls and navigation systems made it easy. We traveled northeast along the string of islands that comprise the upper Keys until we reached the entrance to Biscayne Bay. There were two channels actually; one to the north that brought you close to Stiltsville, and one directly down the center. I would have liked to have gotten close to the stilt houses but took the safer route instead. I called Dinner Key Marina on the radio and listened carefully to their instructions. Somewhat of a harbor lay between small keys and sand bars. This water was full of mooring balls and the moored boats made locating the markers difficult.

I slowed to a crawl and picked my way through the obstacles until I found the entrance channel to the marina. I called again to verify our slip assignment. I saw dockhands scramble to assist us. The rich folks really do get special treatment. Brody tossed lines and shouted instructions to the guys on the dock. I assisted with the engines and bow thruster until we were snugly secured. I was happy to have not made a fool of myself. I'd actually made a pretty smooth landing.

"Good job, Breeze," said Brody.

"Good job, mate," I said.

This was where we normally told *Miss Leap* she'd done a good job. We looked at each other and shrugged. As far as we knew, the boat didn't have a name yet.

"Good job, *Incognito*," I said. "Or whatever your name is."

After we got cleaned up, Brody tried the marina's Wi-Fi. Like most marinas the signal was weak. She carried her stuff up to the dayroom to try to get a better signal. I worked with the GPS to lay in a course to St. Croix. We were still over a thousand miles away. I did some rough calculations. Our vessel's range and speed left plenty of room for error. We'd make it in two days if we ran nonstop at twenty-five knots. That was assuming Brody was up to the task. She hadn't gotten behind the helm of this particular vessel yet. I could coach her through it; after all, the autopilot would do most of the work. I planned a fuel stop about halfway just to be safe.

I wondered again about marinas down there. I ambled up the docks to find Brody and see if she'd made any progress.

"I set up a bogus email account and sent a message to Fred," she said. "Haven't heard back yet. The signal is still lame even up here. I'm having trouble with the vendor websites. It would be easier just to call them."

"Let's go find another disposable phone," I said. "This close to Miami it ought to be big business."

We walked out to the busy street and looked both ways. There was a Mobil station two blocks away. Half the signs were written in Spanish. Cubans loitered out back with bottles of beer in brown paper bags. Posh Coconut Grove was just a few blocks away, but we could have been in Havana. There was a rack of pre-paid phone cards on the counter. The phones themselves were under glass. Brody made the transaction, selecting an hour's worth of talk time. The clerk rang us up and wished us a nice day.

We went back to the dayroom. There was still no reply from Fred. We called him but got no answer.

"I'll use this crappy Wi-Fi to bring up the websites," she said. "Find the phone numbers that I need."

"I'll go get a notebook and a pen," I said.

It seemed ludicrous that we were on a multi-million dollar yacht, in a fancy marina, yet we couldn't properly use the internet. We needed a smartphone with a hotspot, but we couldn't risk being discovered. I was certain that we were safe for the time being. We hadn't mentioned this destination on any phone or computer. Our only communication had been by VHF radio. Unless they followed us by helicopter they couldn't possibly know where we were and we hadn't seen any helicopters.

Brody ran out of time. It was too late in the day to contact the offices of the various suppliers she wanted to speak with. Our great humanitarian mission was not off to a splendid start. We were both frustrated with the situation. We considered canceling the whole thing. I was worried that if we sat in one spot for too long, we'd be tracked down somehow. There was still no word from Fred. That made us worry some more. To distract ourselves we went out for a nice dinner. We found Le Bouchon Du Grove in the middle of Coconut Grove. It was one of those goat cheese, pate, and foie gras places. I got the Chilean Sea Bass and Brody chose a filet. With drinks, the meal came to a hundred bucks. For the area we were in, I suppose we got off easy. I pictured fried chicken or meatloaf cooked in our country kitchen.

We skipped dessert and walked the water-front. I squeezed her hand and pointed to my eyes. Stay alert girl. We took in the sights and sounds and saw nothing suspicious. The boat's security system was also on alert, though we had no device to monitor it from. We should have heard back from Fred by now. The fact that he hadn't contacted us got more worrisome by the minute. We approached his boat carefully, wary of anything out of place. There were no alarms going off or any other sign of intruders. We locked ourselves inside and spent some time watching all the camera feeds. Nothing was out of place. No strangers were watching. We double-checked our weapons for no particular reason. We were prisoners of our paranoia.

I couldn't sleep. I lay there in bed with my doubts and fears. I wanted to fulfill the commitment I'd made to render aid in St. Croix, but it was making less sense with each passing day. I was afraid that something had happened to Captain Fred. It was my job to keep his boat safe. Where would it be safest? Here, or St. Croix, or somewhere else? It was also my job to keep Brody safe. I'd dragged her off on another silly quest and put her in harm's way yet again. When would I ever learn? I kept turning it over in my head until I convinced myself that it would be best to continue with our aid mission to St. Croix. No one could know where we were going. It would be the safest thing to do and I could still keep my promise. I felt like the scales of karma had shifted somewhat in my favor. I'd made up for some of my wrongdoings. If I could just do this one last thing, I'd feel better about it and I'd feel better about myself. I could retire from this life knowing that I'd done some good on the way out. After I'd settled the argument with myself, I was able to get some rest.

The next morning brought no news from Fred. I told Brody about my decision. After breakfast, we went back to the dayroom to continue the process of trying to get supplies. I left it all up to Brody. She worked the phone for most of the day. She learned that by mentioning the relief mission that she got more attention. She got calls back from superiors, wanting to know how they could help. The logistics of delivery was the biggest issue, but Brody kept after them until arrangements were made. I calculated available square footage inside the boat. We made estimates of how much of each product we could store. She kept making calls until we figured we'd have a full load. It was great progress. Instead of celebrating with another fancy dinner, we ordered pizza from Domino's. A six-pack from the Mobil station rounded out our fare for the evening.

Darkness fell with no word from Fred. We couldn't wait for him. We had shit to do. We'd have to do it without reliable internet.

Most of the work was done, thanks to Brody and a twenty dollar phone. We spent the next several days taking deliveries and stocking the boat. We spent way too much money on the merchandise, delivery fees, and taking care of the people who brought it to us. By the end of the week, the boat was crammed full. We'd managed to make a reservation at Green Cay Marina on the east end of St. Croix. It was time to cast off.

We filled up with fuel and water and some groceries for ourselves. The weather was stable. We cruised back across Biscayne Bay and out into the Atlantic. We shot across the Gulf Stream with no difficulty. The big boat plowed through the current with ease. We ran straight to Nassau. It was good to be on the move. We'd seen nothing suspicious in Dinner Key, but there was no point in tempting fate. We spent one night in Nassau and continued south through the Exumas, stopping at Emerald Bay again for fuel. We were completely out of touch. We had no communications whatsoever. If Fred had tried to contact us, we didn't know about it. We'd check again at the next marina.

For each leg of the trip, I'd start out behind the helm. When we got a position where the autopilot could take over for an extended period, Brody would take my place and I'd catch a quick nap when necessary. Brody did the same. We arrived in St. Croix after three days at sea. Green Cay Marina had only one spot large enough for us. We waited while they rearranged some boats to make room. Brody scrambled off to check her email while I checked on the ship's systems. She'd done fine so far. It had been a nice break-in period for her. We hadn't pushed her too hard. Everything held together and operated within normal ranges. Hatteras had done a great job making her ready.

I joined Brody outside the marina office.

"Nothing from Fred," she said. "I'll call the charity group that's supposed to take this stuff off our hands."

"Try Fred's phone again," I said.

There was still no answer. She left a message. The Community Association of the V.I. was happy to hear of our arrival. They'd send trucks and plenty of help in the morning. Our mission was all but over, just like that.

"What do we do next?" asked Brody. "Where do we go?"

"I guess stay here for a while," I said. "Hope Fred gets in touch."

"Will we be safe here?" she asked.

My first thought was that there was no way anyone could know where we were, but that nagging feeling hit me at the same time. Had we left any clues behind? Were we being tracked somehow? If so, they'd have hit us at Dinner Key. I could think of nothing that we'd done that would reveal our whereabouts, but that gut feeling wouldn't go away.

Eleven

Trucks and work crews arrived the next day to relieve us of our supplies. A caravan of hand trucks and dock carts moved back and forth on the docks. I was preoccupied with the menial task of lifting and lugging boxes. I was not alert to my surroundings. That was a big mistake.

I was handing a heavy item up to a helper on the truck when an explosion went off in the back of my head. I saw a bright flash of light before the pain took over. I never saw what hit me. I was on the ground on my hands and knees. I stared at a rock that wouldn't come into focus. I didn't know where I was. Movement was impossible. I heard the sound of Brody's gun. She fired off two shots in quick succession. Blap, Blap.

Next, I took a tremendous blow to the ribs. I heard them crack. They were the same ribs that had been broken previously by an angry hammerhead shark. The pain was intense. It combined with the pain in my head and made me nauseous. I couldn't breathe. I lay there gasping, tasting my own vomit. Two more shots rang out. The caveman fell on top of me. I knew I was in real trouble. His weight was crushing. I couldn't get any air. I realized at that moment what I'd been trying to grasp all along. I'd searched the internet for marinas in St. Croix. There was only one that could accommodate us. I'd led him right to us. Now it was time to pay for that dreadful mistake. I was sorely in need of oxygen. Time was running out for me.

I heard Brody grunting as she worked to roll the caveman off of me. Others pitched in and I was freed. I couldn't move or speak. Then I blacked out. I don't recall much of what happened after that other than what Brody told me later. I was unaware of the world outside my own mind. They say that when you are near death, your life passes before your eyes. That is not what I saw. I saw only death.

I saw my grandfather wailing as they closed the lid to my grandmother's casket. I saw him lying in that same funeral home just a short time later. I saw my mother in bed at her home. I sat with her during her final moments. She was drugged up to ease the pain of cancer. When her time came, she did not simply close her eyes and stop breathing. She spasmed violently with a look of terror in her eyes. That moment haunted me until I was able to erase it from my memory. Now it came back to me in vivid detail. These were not dreams. They were exact replays of events, played back to taunt me.

I saw my older sister. I loaded her into a hospice ambulance so she could die at home in peace. She was only fifty years old. She'd been a good friend to me. I saw my father in a hospital bed in Maine. I saw the tears in his eyes when I told him how proud I was to be his son. These were things that I didn't think about. I'd buried all the loss and agony deep down where I wouldn't have to deal with it ever again. I was angry about having it all brought to the forefront, but I could do nothing to resist.

I saw my wife Laura, her lifeless body was in that hospital bed in Maryland. It shattered me anew. I still thought of her from time to time. It made me feel guilty for moving on, but I had no other choice. I ran as far away from that time as I could manage. I saw Joy. I held her in my arms as she drew her last breath. Her blood soaked my clothing. I ran through the streets of Miami like a madman. I kept running from her death for a long time after.

I saw myself, beating Bobbie Beard to death in the Guatemalan jungle. I'd replayed that fateful act in my head a thousand times. I knew how it ended. Why was I seeing death? What was the message? Is that all there is? One minute you're alive and then you're gone? Reliving those moments was torturous. Was it a punishment? Was I already dead? I did not wish to be dead.

Finally, I saw Brody. She was not dead. That made me happy. I thought that if I was indeed dead, I'd miss her very much. She'd given meaning to my life. I learned that I could care for someone in a way that I thought I was no longer capable of. She was sitting next to me and holding my hand. Her eyes sparkled and she smiled at me. She was telling me that I was going to be okay. She told me that she loved me. Then I realized that I had regained consciousness. Brody was real. I was not dead after all. I tried to smile back at her. Nothing happened at first. I took stock of my body. My head hurt. I had a piercing sensation on one side of my chest. I moved my eyes to look around the room as best I could. Brody squeezed my hand and moved in closer.

"I'm alive," I whispered.

"Of course you are," she said. "I never had a doubt."

"Where am I?"

"St. Thomas," she said. "But don't exert yourself. Let me get the doctor."

The doctor came in and did an examination. He shined a light into my eyes and moved his finger back and forth. I followed it the best I could. He pinched my fingers and toes. I could feel it each time. He listened to my heart and lungs. He didn't have much to say. That was okay with me. I didn't have much to say myself. I still wasn't fully aware of what was going on. I only knew that I was alive, and I intended to stay that way. After the doctor left, Brody explained my condition in layman's terms.

"The blow to your head caused swelling of the brain," she said. "They had to drill a hole in your skull. You've also got a punctured lung. You underwent surgery and there's a tube in your chest."

I slowly moved one arm up to my face. There was plastic tubing under my nose.

"Oxygen," she said. "You're working on one lung for the time being, and your brain needs more oxygen too."

"I'm a mess," I said.

"You should have seen the other guy," she said.

"The caveman?"

"He's dead," she informed me. "Took four shots to stop him."

"You okay?"

"Don't you worry about me," she said. "I'm just fine. It's you who needs to be taken care of this time."

"Thank you," I said. "You saved my life."

"You would have done the same," she said. "Sorry you had to get all busted up."

"Me too."

That was all I could take. I was out again for a long time. There were no more visions of death. The caveman didn't come for me in my dreams. Bobby Beard left me alone too.

Over the next week, I stayed awake for longer and longer periods. Nurses and doctors came and went, but Brody always seemed to be there. Bandages were changed frequently. The chest tube was removed. There was a big moment when I stood up for the first time. I immediately got dizzy but managed to stay standing for a full minute. My head still ached. My ribs were still painful. Soon enough I could walk around the room a little bit. They took me off the oxygen machine and gave me a little bottle to wheel around with me. I was weak and easily confused. I had no idea what day or time it was at any given moment. I'd forgotten why we were in the Virgin Islands in the first place. I knew that it had been important for me to get here and that my zeal had brought down misery on us both. I'd been sentenced to a hospital bed for my transgressions. I'd missed an important clue. I'd let my guard down. I failed at the very thing I was best at. It was clear that I was on the back side of life's mountain. It was all downhill from there. I'd seen the signs that I was slowing down and losing my edge. Now this was proof.

I resigned myself to a slower life in the mountains of North Carolina. At least I had that to look forward to. Me and the other old farts would meet at the country store every Thursday to talk sports and bitch about our wives. I'd whittle doodads on the back porch and feed the squirrels. I'd hide bottles of moonshine around the property so I could take a nip whenever Brody wasn't looking. I'd take up smoking a pipe. I'd sit in the recliner wearing a big wool sweater and slippers. I'd forget all about drug runners and treasure hunters. I'd trade white sand for a white

Christmas. I'd grow older and slower and more harmless as each year passed.

I was feeling pretty sorry for myself, but I didn't let it slow my rehab. I did as I was instructed. I took my pills and breathed into the little machine four times daily. I walked further and further each time out. Soon enough I was ready to be released. I wished I could be magically transported to that cabin in the woods, but there was Fred's boat to take care of and my own boat back in Florida. Whatever happened to Fred anyway? As my body healed my mind started to come around as well. Fred was AWOL. I didn't know what that meant or what I could do about it in my present condition.

There was also the possibility that Fred's boat was a death trap for us. The caveman had failed but that didn't mean more men wouldn't come for us. I couldn't
expect Brody to take care of the boat and our safety by herself. I felt helpless. I relayed my concerns to Brody.

"I've just been concentrating on you getting better," she said. "I don't know what we're supposed to do now."

"We can't pay for that slip forever," I said. "We've got to get out of here eventually."

"We're also paying for *Miss Leap's* slip," she reminded me. "Fred has left us in a pickle."

"He wouldn't do it on purpose," I said. "Something is wrong."

"Let's get you out of here for now," she said. "See how you fare on the boat. One step at a time."

I moved back onto Fred's boat and continued the healing process. My pain level had been greatly reduced, but I had little energy or stamina. I could handle normal activity, but nothing strenuous. I was going a bit stir crazy. I was polishing some stainless one day when a stranger appeared on the dock below me. I hadn't seen him around. He wasn't part of the marina staff.

"Excuse me, sir," he said. "I have mail for you."

I came down and he handed me a letter. He turned and walked away. I took the letter inside and found Brody. I opened the envelope. It was a ransom letter.

Mr. and Mrs. Breeze,

Your good friend Fred Ford is in our custody. We do not wish to cause him harm, but it remains a possibility. His fate lies in your hands. We hereby demand that you deliver his vessel to us in exchange for his life. We will release him to your custody once we are in possession of the vessel and all of its contents.

You have forty-eight hours to comply. We have reserved dockage for you in Tortola. Take the first left beyond the cruise ship docks. Space will be available for you on the starboard side. We will have men there to greet you.

Don't worry about your weapons. You will be outmanned and outgunned. Failure to comply with this demand will result in the death of your friend. His blood will be on your hands.

The letter was not signed. We both read through it again. It was straightforward if nothing else. Deliver the boat or Fred dies. I was in no physical or mental shape to attempt to concoct a rescue plan. We had no choice but to comply.

At least it solved our dilemma about what to do with Fred's boat. Brody agreed with my assessment.

"Are you up to driving this thing over there?" she asked.

"It's not far," I said. "We'll be there in a few hours."

"Could we hire someone to deliver it for us?"

"We have to be there to get Fred," I said. "We can't just leave him there alone. He doesn't know where we are and we can't communicate with him."

"What if it's a trap?"

"They haven't been after us all along," I said. "They want this boat or something on this boat. At least they think something important is onboard. They were just using us to get to Fred."

"Then why did the caveman attack you with such vengeance?"

"Probably because we outsmarted him back in Fort Myers," I said.

"I know you're not a hundred percent," she said. "But what's your gut telling you?"

"They just want the boat," I said. "They'll give us Fred. They've already lost one man. They want it to end."

"I hope you're right," she said. "Why Tortola I wonder?"

"It's not a U.S. territory," I guessed. "Lots of yachts in that harbor from all over the world. Fred's boat won't raise any suspicion at all."

We spent the rest of the afternoon packing our few belongings. We put our weapons in the backpacks with the rest of our stuff, unloaded. Brody cooked us a decent meal. We sat out back and pondered our coexistence.

"Looks like this is the end of the road," Brody said. "By the time we get home, it will be time to move to the cabin, assuming we get home that is."

"The last adventure," I said. "The way this has turned out makes retirement seem like a really good idea."

"I hear you," she said. "I'm going to have to get awfully bored before I'd want to do this again."

"I'm sorry for letting you down," I said. "I've always been able to count on my wits to win the day. Looks like that's over now."

"Stop with the pity party," she said. "It's long past time that you quit this life. You've got a woman who loves you and a sweet little cabin in the hills. Doesn't sound so bad to me."

"You're right, as usual," I said. "It does sound quite nice."

We hadn't made love since I'd been battered and broken by the caveman. We approached it gently and slowly. Brody was so tender it almost made me cry. I loved her more than ever. The ending to my nautical life was bittersweet. I loved the boats and the waters and it was hard to believe I was leaving that all behind. I had Brody though. We'd make each other happy no matter where we went. I had the rest of my life to spend with her, away from the violence and stress that resulted from my choices here. It was time. I knew it then.

We were both nervous the next morning as we prepared the boat to leave the dock. It was a relatively short hop from St. Croix to Tortola. The worry was about what we'd find when we arrived. Either we'd turn over the boat and reunite with Captain Fred, or we'd meet our maker. I was rooting for the first option. I let the engines warm up more than necessary, hesitant to leave. Brody was pacing back and forth.

"It's now or never," I said.

"Let's do this," she answered. "Get it over with."

We untied from the dock and eased away. No great navigational skills were necessary. You could pilot by sight to most of the islands nearby. The water was very deep so there was no chance of running aground. Once we were clear of the harbor I ran the throttles all the way forward. She rose up on plane and cut a sharp path through the water. I ran her hard for ten minutes just to see what she could do. Our speed topped out at thirty-five knots. I eased her back down to a comfortable cruising speed. This would be the last time I'd get to be her pilot. She had exceeded all of my expectations over the time I'd spend at her helm. I realized that this might be the last time I'd drive any boat, not just this one. It was a sobering realization.

I just wouldn't be the same person without a boat. I'd be losing my identity. I'd have to create a new one. Mountain Breeze had a nice ring to it. If I were going to make this change, I needed to embrace it. Maybe Mountain Breeze could find some new adventures up there in North Carolina.

Twelve

We approached the harbor entrance for Tortola. A massive cruise ship was docked to our port. I crawled past it and took the first left. This was the commercial section of the harbor. Fishing boats, ferries and tour boats lined the docks. To my starboard was a long stretch of empty dock. That was for me. Three men sat on a bench midway down the dock. When they saw me they stood up. That was my greeting committee. I didn't see Captain Fred. I approached slowly and carefully. Brody went down to toss lines. Once we were secured, I went down below and grabbed our backpacks.

One of the men boarded us.

"I'll just have a quick look around and then we'll take you to your friend," he said.

We waited onboard until he finished his inspection. When he was finished he motioned for us to disembark. We obeyed. They led us off the dock into the parking lot. The doors of a black SUV opened. Fred got out along with a tall, well-dressed gentleman. Fred looked forlorn in his disheveled clothing. His hair was messed up and he was lacking his ever-present cigar. The tall man was neat as a pin in his expensive suit. We all just stood there looking at each other until the tall man spoke.

"You have made the proper decision," he said. "I will honor my word. The three of you are free to go."

We looked at each other and shrugged. We had nowhere to go but we needed to get out of there.

"You can take a taxi to the airport," said the tall man. "Have a nice afternoon."

There we stood, three stranded travelers, standing in a parking lot alongside Tortola Harbor. The tall man and his crew went to Fred's boat. I'd been here before. Laura and I chartered a catamaran from The Moorings on the opposite side of the basin. I'd proposed to her on our first night out, while moored off Cooper Island. We'd spent the best week of our lives island hopping, drinking too much and making love every day. Years later, I returned with her ashes to spread on the beach at Norman Island. Standing there that day brought back all those memories. I knew we could get a ride to the airport at the Moorings base. I directed Brody and Fred to follow me.

I didn't get far before I was out of breath. I had to sit down and rest. My head and ribs were aching and I couldn't get enough air.

"I might be worse for wear," said Fred. "But you look like hell. What happened?"

"A goon who works for your associates down there tried to break me in half," I said. "Damn near succeeded. Brody was forced to take him out."

"Where'd this happen?" he asked.

"St. Croix," I told him. "That's where we took your boat to hide out. Didn't work."

"Jesus Christ what a mess I've made," he said. "I sincerely apologize for getting you involved."

"Sorry about your boat," I said. "I was in no shape to mount any type of counteroffensive."

"He's lucky to be alive," Brody chimed in. "I guess you are too. They threatened to kill you if we didn't deliver the boat. We had no choice."

"I get it," said Fred. "Nothing much else you could've done, but damn, I wish I'd gotten to spend a few hours on that thing. Sure was a beautiful yacht."

"What are you going to do now?" I asked him.

"I'll report it stolen," he said. "Insurance will pay out. Unless they dismantle every last piece of the security system you installed, I'll be able to track it. Most likely it will be recovered someday."

"Which brings us to the big question," I said. "Why did they want it so badly?"

"I'm not even sure who the hell they are," he said. "Not the same bunch we dealt with in the Bahamas. I'm assuming they think I've got some proprietary technology stashed aboard, but I swear, I don't."

"You've barely stepped foot on her," I said. "Could it be something else?"

"Obviously I've made enemies," he said. "Maybe they just want to dick with me. Make me miserable. Make me pay for some perceived injustice somewhere along the line."

"They had you in custody," I said. "They could have extracted their justice on your hide if they'd wanted to."

"They didn't torture me or anything like that," he said. "It wasn't comfortable, and I'm starving, but otherwise they didn't hurt me."

"Let's find something to eat," Brody suggested.

I made it the rest of the way to the Moorings base but barely. I sat at the outside bar and ordered three painkillers from the bartender. I suggested that he make them strong. Chicken was cooking on a grill under the cabana. Charter customers lounged by the pool, awaiting delivery of their yacht for the week. We weren't vacationers. Brody and I had our backpacks. Fred had his wallet and passport. The painkillers worked their magic. We all took plates of chicken with plantains and rice and ate in the shade.

"So some random organization with the surveillance powers of the NSA tracked us halfway around the world so they could steal your boat," I said. "Then, instead of simply disposing of us they kidnap you. Use the boat as ransom in exchange for your freedom."

"Something like that," he said.

"Where were you when they nabbed you?"

"Cartagena," he said.

"How'd they know where to find you?" I asked. "I thought your communications were secure."

"Through someone else who called me I suppose," he said. "They'd have to eavesdrop on a wide circle to finally hit on the right person."

"Then that was probably us," I said. "It's been us the whole time. Our damn devices led them to you."

"I'm afraid you may be right," he said. "I guess I relied on your relative anonymity to shield you from something like that."

"Brody and I became a lot less anonymous because of that whole FBI fiasco," I said. "Our names likely went into every database in D.C. afterward."

"These guys had the right connections to access that information," he said.

"Wouldn't surprise me if someone in D.C. sold us out," said Brody. "I didn't make any friends up there."

"I did," I said. "Troy with Enduring Warrior. He's got contacts with military intelligence. I could call him. Maybe flush out who exposed us."

"Stop right there, Breeze," said Brody. "You'll do no such thing. We're going to slip out of Florida and go to our cabin in the woods. We're leaving all of this nonsense behind. We won't have a phone or a computer. We'll pay for everything in cash. No one will ever know where we are."

"Sorry," I said. "Old habits and all."

"Wait just a damn minute," said Fred. "What's this about a cabin in the woods? You're leaving the water?"

"*Leap of Faith* is for sale," I told him. "We're leaving very soon. We've decided on a change of pace. This life is going to get one of us killed sooner or later."

"I never thought I'd see the day," he said. "How will I get in touch with you?"

I didn't have the heart to tell him he'd never hear from us again. He and I went way back.

We'd helped each other multiple times over the years. He'd been a good friend and benefactor to me. I'd done my best to return the favor.

"Give us time to get settled," I said. "We'll do the burner phone thing to check in from time to time."

"I'm going to miss having you around, my friend," he said.

"I'll miss you too, Fred," I said. "But I won't miss having the bad guys shooting at me or trying to crush my skull."

"I never intended for things to work out that way," he said. "Got too big for my britches I suppose. Maybe it's time for me to disappear too."

"Enjoy your money, captain," I said. "Life is short."

"My plan is to live forever," he said. "So far, so good."

We finished up our meals, had one last round of painkillers, and got the bartender to hail us a cab to the airport on Beef Island. We had not officially checked in with Customs when we arrived so there was a hassle. After paying a small departure tax we were waved through.

We quickly learned that we'd missed the last flight to San Juan for the day. No more flights were leaving for St. Thomas either. If the guy at the Customs desk had told us that, we could have gone back to town and found a room. By this time, we were all exhausted. We found spots to sit down and settled in for a long night of nothing. Beef Island isn't like a modern American airport. A dog lay on the cool floor by the departures gate. Pigeons roosted in the open rafters. We watched the last arriving flight land just before dark. There was a very small bar and a couple of little stores, all closed. There was no television in the waiting area. When it came time to lie down, we had to do it on the floor.

There was no breakfast available in the morning, but we were able to get three seats on the first flight to San Juan. A new customs agent tried to hit us up for a second departure fee. We had our receipts from the previous day. We walked out onto the tarmac to board the small prop plane. There were only two other passengers. The flight attendant positioned us to equally distribute our weight. The flight was a short one, thankfully and we were deposited into the busy terminal at the San Juan airport.

Captain Fred took charge here. He was a pro in airports and could throw his weight and influence around. He booked us first class seats to Fort Myers, paying for them with his credit card.

"Where will you go, Fred?" I asked.

"I've still got a house in central Florida," he said. "I'll regroup there. Deal with the insurance on both boats. Tend to my business."

"How's it feel to go from being a two boat owner to not having either one?"

"Damn strange," he said. "I'm not the least bit happy about it. It's a crying shame what happened to *Incognito*. Never got to know the new one. I've got half a mind to retaliate."

"Against who?"

"That boat's going to turn up sooner or later," he said. "Someone will try to sell it, or use it to run drugs. I'll get a lead on it somehow."

"Then what? Steal it back?"

"Right now I'm more concerned with punishing whoever is responsible," he said.

"But the wound is still open. I'll think it through more rationally after I get home."

"Neither one of us is getting any younger," I said. "Maybe it's time for us both to step back."

"You get older by acting older," he said. "You sit on your couch and yell at the kids to get off your lawn. You watch TV all day and start taking Geritol. That ain't for me."

"Have it your way," I said. "But I plan to sit on my porch and watch the wildlife. Put out some hummingbird feeders. Toss corn to the squirrels."

"You'll be bored out of your mind," he said. "Call me when you can't take it anymore."

The flight was a pleasant one. We touched down in Fort Myers late afternoon. Fred arranged for a car to take us to the marina. We parted ways when it arrived.

"Take care of yourself," I said. "It's been good to call you friend."

"Likewise, son," he said. "If you ever need anything, don't hesitate to get in touch."

I had the feeling the Fred would catch the next plane to someplace exotic and plot his revenge. I wanted no part in it. I still needed more time to recover from the beating I'd taken. North Carolina was sounding better and better.

The limo ride back to the marina would be our last taste of Fred's generosity, and it was greatly appreciated. I helped myself to some fancy champagne, lay back in the cushy seat and tried to decompress. We'd done some good in this world over the past few months. Some folks down in Puerto Rico and St. John would benefit from our efforts, but it had ended in disaster. Fred was out two fine yachts. I was physically damaged far worse than I'd ever been in my life. We'd blown several hundred thousand of our life's savings. Worst of all, our spirits were deflated. My ego was hurt too, but I'd get over that eventually. All the signs were there. Our time in Florida needed to end. There'd be no looking back.

We knew something was wrong as soon as we got out of the limo. The air was foul with the smell of dead fish. Our eyes immediately began to burn. By the time we walked to the boat, our throats were irritated too. The water in the marina basin was thick with dead grass and sea life.

"What the hell happened here?" asked Brody.

"Probably Red Tide," I said. "A particularly bad one."

"It's disgusting," she said. "We can't stay here."

It was better inside the boat with the air conditioner running. The last thing I wanted to do was drive to some hotel. All I wanted to do was vegetate. I grabbed a beer and turned on the television, something I rarely did. The local news was reporting on a multitude of local water quality issues. A massive bloom of Red Tide was centered over our area. Scenes from Boca Grande looked like a nuclear bomb had exploded. The beach was lined with thousands of dead fish of all species. Huge grouper and tarpon swelled in the heat. A dead manatee was decomposing near the phosphate docks. Mullet, trout, snook, and crabs were all present in equal numbers. Even Cayo Costa had been affected. Signs warning of poor air quality had been posted on Manasota Key. There were no-swim advisories from Sanibel to Venice.

Meanwhile, a thick river of blue-green algae was approaching the Gulf. It had been released through the floodgates of Lake Okeechobee and into the Caloosahatchee River. Waterfowl glowed fluorescent green. Manatees struggled to breathe. Shell beds close to the coast were smothered. A double whammy of destruction was attacking southwest Florida. Tourism faltered. Waterfront restaurants had no customers. Locals who had waited patiently for the snowbirds to leave now couldn't enjoy the beaches. It was a sad thing to see. Those waters had been not only my home but my sustenance. They were a part of me. Seeing the devastation made me physically ill like I'd lost a loved one.

The stupidity of man should never be underestimated. Most all of the factors causing the decline of Florida's water quality were due to man's stupid decisions. Choices were made generations ago that we now paying the price for.

In the 1910s, a small earthen dike was constructed around much of Lake Okeechobee. This containment was breached by the storm surge from the Great Miami Hurricane in 1926. It was totally destroyed during the 1928 Okeechobee Hurricane, killing thousands. After these disasters, the Florida legislature created the Okeechobee Flood Control District, which was authorized to cooperate with the U.S. Army Corps of Engineers in flood control undertakings.

After a personal inspection from President Herbert Hoover, the Corps drafted a new plan which provided for the construction of floodway channels, control gates, and major levees along the Lake's shores. A long-term system was designed for the purpose of flood control, water conservation, and saltwater intrusion. Draining the swamp was the goal. Politicians and developers wanted to create more land for development and agriculture. A huge portion of the Everglades was lost as a result.

Some knuckleheads in Tallahassee decided that the Kissimmee River needed to be straightened so that it could more efficiently carry run-off from the Orlando area into Lake

O. No longer was the tainted water filtered by the marshes on the river banks. No longer did the River of Grass filter runoff from Lake O before it made it to the Gulf. Other assholes decided to dig a canal to connect the big lake directly to the Caloosahatchee River, something Mother Nature never intended.

Later, the newly formed land below the dike became home to America's largest sugar producers. Small towns sprung up to support the cane field workers. The sugar operations began a process known as "back pumping" whenever there was too much water in the fields. The nutrient-rich and fertilizer-laden water helped algae blooms in the lake to explode. Over time, the algae blooms grew toxic. That didn't stop the state of Florida from releasing a poisonous goo into both the Caloosahatchee and the St. Lucie Rivers. Those sugar barons also polluted the politics of Florida. Millions of dollars were donated to the campaigns of both parties. It didn't matter who won the election. It didn't matter who controlled the state government. Big Sugar always had friends in power.

Charlotte Harbor had once been the center of this country's phosphate business. The stuff was mined on the Peace River and brought to Boca Grande to be loaded onto ships. The phosphate industry died, but it left a legacy of environmental damage behind. All of these factors combined to degrade our waterways and they were all influenced by one thing; rainfall.

During the winter in south Florida, it almost never rains. Months can go by without a drop. The water levels in Lake O drop considerably, sometimes even causing a hazard to navigation. The lack of runoff from Lake O and the Peace River allows the nearshore waters of the Gulf to clear. All winter long the snowbirds enjoy crystal water and pristine beaches. Fishing is good. Tourism abounds.

Sometime around June first it starts to rain. It will continue to rain nearly every day throughout the summer months. South Florida gets as much rainfall in six months as the Amazon rainforest gets in a year. Lake O fills up and threatens the integrity of the dike. The water has to be released. Before man screwed it all up, it simply flowed over the southern banks and into the Everglades. It worked well for millions of years. The ecosystem of the Glades was rich and diverse. It was home to rookeries of hundreds of bird species. It provided the nesting grounds for another hundred species of fish. All that has been negatively affected by the decisions that man has made. Now saltwater intrudes further inland than it ever has. The swamp is starved for fresh water. Florida Bay is out of balance as well as both coasts. The Peace River swells during the rainy season as well. Water floods the banks and is contaminated by the phosphate-laden soil. Tannin from the mangroves stains it a dark brown. It flows heavily into Charlotte Harbor and out to the Gulf via the Boca Grande Pass.

Wildlife, especially fish, pay the ultimate price, but so do seabirds, turtles, and the manatee. Don't get me wrong, Red Tide and algae blooms are naturally occurring, but I can't help but feel that man has done everything he can to exacerbate the problem and there appears to be zero political will to attempt to fix it. It was one more reason to give up on life in southwest Florida. I was so done with all of it. It was almost humorous how fast my mind had changed, but events and circumstances had conspired to make me want to run away as fast as possible. It had been a good phase in my life. At times it had been fantastic. Now it was over.

Thirteen

Back when I first bought *Leap of Faith*, the owners of the brokerage I used were good to me. They helped me through the process in a friendly way. They didn't blink when I wanted to pay with cash. I decided to call on them to help me sell her. Greg came to the marina to fill out the paperwork and take a bunch of pictures. He advised me on the boat's true value, which was less than I had hoped for. I didn't need the extra money, I just didn't want her to feel cheap. She was worth much more to me in a sentimental way, but I needed her gone. I couldn't take care of her from North Carolina. We were soon to leave Florida and I wouldn't be available to show her to prospective buyers. I put my trust in Greg and moved on from it.

Brody was beside herself with excitement about our upcoming new life. We had a bedroom suite and a sofa in storage. She was constantly shopping, mostly to get ideas on furniture and décor for a cabin. Her search was hampered by my disdain for the internet. We couldn't simply fill our Amazon cart and pay by credit card. She did use her Kindle to browse. She could pick up a weak signal at the pool and spent hours every day scanning the web for cabin stuff.

I busied myself making sure *Miss Leap* was as clean and mechanically sound as possible. I scrubbed the decks and applied a new coat of sealer. I touched up some blemished brightwork. I offloaded anything that wasn't absolutely necessary. Some I threw away. Some went into storage. I could only work in short bursts. I still suffered from shortness of breath. The heat was brutal. I could manage twenty minutes outdoors at a time before retreating to the air conditioning to cool off and rehydrate. My head hurt less but would act up when I had to put it down to perform some chore. The bad air quality hampered my breathing. I had frequent coughing fits when

I'd feel like I was hacking up a lung. Brody was concerned about my breathing.

"All I need is a little fresh mountain air," I told her.

I wasn't so sure. Something didn't feel right with my lungs. The coughing fits worsened. I really needed to get out of there. If I told Brody the truth, she'd haul me off to a doctor. I wasn't going to let anything get in the way of our move. If I didn't improve in the cleaner air, I'd deal with it later.

Our soured attitude towards Florida did not improve. The last few days passed very slowly. Finally, we loaded our small collection of furniture and a meager amount of belongings onto a U Haul truck and started making our way north. We stopped in Columbia again, staying at the same hotel we got on the first trip to North Carolina.

"One more day," I told Brody. "We'll be there tomorrow early in the afternoon."

"There's so much to do," she said. "We'll need to get more furniture right away."

"We'll unload what we have, go out for a nice dinner, and start looking the following day," I said. "It doesn't all have to happen overnight."

"I know, I'm just so excited," she said. "A real home. I hope you know what this means to me."

"It means everything to me to make you happy," I said. "You've been a real trooper on the boat. Never complained. I appreciate that, but it will be nice to make a home together on land."

"Admit it," she said. "You're looking forward to this as much as I am."

"Sure I am," I said. "After what we've been through lately, the peace and solitude will be welcome."

I'd had stretches of peace and solitude from time to time living on a boat, but I was mostly alone. Brody and I had a year of it down in the Caribbean but found ourselves longing for civilization. That's how we ended up in a marina instead of on the hook constantly. We'd enjoyed the amenities and the safety, but the proximity to so many people soon got on our nerves. I'd developed some kind of social anxiety. Trying to maintain constant awareness wore me out. Being alert to the potential danger that may or may not ever come was tiring. It reached its crest down there in St. Croix. I'd made critical mistakes. I couldn't keep it up forever.

I hoped the cabin would provide the type of sanctuary I needed. No one knew where it was except the log home builder. We'd paid him in cash. We even lied to the U Haul clerk about our destination. We'd left no forwarding address. I told the yacht broker that I'd check in with him every few months. If the boat sold he could hang onto the money until he heard from me.

We made it up to the cabin just after noon the following day. We did a quick walk-through before unloading the truck. It was even better than we'd remembered. We stood in the middle of the open living area and hugged for a long time.

"This is so awesome, Breeze," Brody said. "We're going to love it here."

"I want to go down to the creek before we start working," I said. "Come with me."

We walked hand in hand down the gently sloping yard to the edge of the creek. I stood close to the bank and watched the clear mountain water stream by. The sound of the running water was soothing music to my soul. I searched the eddies for trout but didn't see any. I pictured myself casting a fly rod at the swirls. I looked up at the taller mountains and took in the view. The temperature was in the mid-seventies on the first day of August. I realized that we needed to buy some warmer clothes soon. An eagle took flight from a nearby pine tree. He circled overhead. I didn't know if it was a welcome or if he was warning me that this was his territory. Mr. Eagle would have to learn to live with old Breeze on his turf. I was going to make this place home.

Together we managed to get our stuff inside. I did have to stop to rest once. The air up there felt somewhat thinner and much less humid than what I was used to. It was indeed easier to breathe, but I simply had not regained my stamina. I sat on the back porch and concentrated on breathing deeply of the crisp mountain air. It definitely helped to rejuvenate me.

The only living room furniture we had was a single couch, but I had to move it three times before Brody was happy with its placement. We worked together to assemble the bed frame with its head and foot boards. The brand new mattress looked inviting. I promised Brody that we'd break it in after dinner. The shower was a good one with plenty of flow and pressure. I stood under the hot water for an extra-long time, because I could.

We drove down the opposite side of the mountain from which we'd arrived and into the small town of Banner Elk. We turned left at the sole traffic light and searched for a decent place to eat. We decided on Stonewalls, a typical American steakhouse. We both selected the prime rib, which was excellent. I was able to enjoy my meal, and Brody's company, without studying every patron and employee, looking for signs of trouble. It was a pleasant change.

Back at the cabin we took our drinks out to the porch and looked out over the property. Squirrels ran in circles around the trunk of an oak tree. A male and female cardinal tended to a single chick. A black snake slithered out from under the porch and wound its way toward the tree line. I guess we disturbed his peace. I looked for the eagle, but he must have been perched out of sight, roosting for the night. We could hear the sound of the creek from the porch. It continued to soothe.

"It's absolutely perfect," Brody whispered. "I am loving you so much right now."

"I'll be loving you in about two minutes," I said. "Let's go."

I took her hand and led her to the bedroom. We undressed in a hurry and slipped under the sheets. There was a newness to our lovemaking that night. Our new start had extended to our sex life. I quite enjoyed the freshness of it. I stared at the ceiling afterward with a big goofy grin on my face. Everything about being there made me feel lighter. The mountain air, the babbling brook, the stillness and serenity of it all was just what the doctor ordered. I fell asleep and dreamed that I was a soaring eagle, master of my mountain domain.

We spent our days furniture shopping. We needed end tables and a coffee table. We needed some lamps and things to hang on the wall. We needed a table and chairs for the dining area. Normally I hated shopping, but this wasn't too bad. Brody was patient with me. If I didn't like something she didn't push it any further. When we both agreed on a particular piece, we bought it and had it delivered. Soon the cabin was furnished to just the right degree. It wasn't too cluttered, but it didn't have awkward empty spaces either. I was happy with it. Brody was always thinking of something else that would improve upon it.

Every morning I walked down to the creek for my daily devotional. That consisted of giving thanks for all that I had. Some days my eagle buddy paid me a visit. I put two chairs and a small table down there and started taking my coffee at creek side. I studied the pools and contours of the banks, watching for trout. I didn't have a rod yet. I wouldn't need one if I never saw any fish.

After walking the property for a month and breathing the clean air, my physical condition improved greatly. We started taking day trips to the assortment of parks in the area. We hiked the trails that I could handle. We located and photographed every waterfall that we could find. We drove up to the ski lodges on Beech and Sugar mountains just to have a drink and look around. We alternated between home-cooked meals and dining at some of the many restaurants in town. The temperature topped out in the upper seventies during the day and cooled into the sixties at night. I made a small fire pit in the backyard. We sat around the fire a few nights a week, just staring into the flames.

I began to tune into the natural sounds we could hear all around the cabin. At first, it just seemed silent, but if you sat still and listened, you could hear a symphony of sounds. Squirrels chattered. Coons fought somewhere out in the woods. Songbirds tweeted their melodies. Hummingbirds drummed their wings like tiny helicopters. Brody had planted some red flowers in boxes on the porch rail and hung feeders for them. They came to grab a snack almost daily. The creek never stopped its murmuring.

We learned that Banner Elk considered itself the Christmas Tree Capital of the World. It was true the pines and firs dominated the woods, but upon closer inspection, I found a variety of other species. Maples, Crape Myrtles and something I couldn't identify grew around the property. I got curious enough to look up the unknown species. It was called a Royal Empress. Off the property, I saw a few willows here and there. Longleaf Pines were everywhere.

I wasn't in Florida anymore. The soil was dark and rich, not sandy. The trees and shrubs were deep green and hardy. Flowers thrived. The grass was thick and healthy but it didn't grow too fast. I hired a local to keep it trimmed for a hundred bucks a month. He came about every ten days or so. It was late summer then. All the flora and fauna was alive and happy.

My breathing had returned to normal. Other than the occasional twitch from my ribs, I wasn't in any pain. My head was fine. I'd been working my legs on our frequent walks. My mind was clear and not preoccupied. I laughed more. I had a much better appetite. My once perpetual tan had faded. I wore long pants and hiking boots most of the time. I did not miss Florida in the least, which surprised both of us.

"Not even a little bit?" asked Brody.

"Never look back," I said. "Other than *Miss Leap* being down there alone, I don't miss a thing."

"I'll check back with you when it's ten degrees with a foot of snow on the ground."

"It will be an adjustment for both of us I'm sure," I said. "We'll get a fire roaring and pile on the blankets."

"So far you seem to be adjusting well," she said. "You seem happier. Not always on edge."

"I'm trying to learn to let it all go," I said. "I've been consciously relaxing and enjoying nature."

"No gators or sharks up here," she said. "Bears probably. You seen any yet?"

"I have not," I said. "But I'm sure they are out there in the hills someplace."

"What do we do if one comes onto the property?" she asked.

"Keep the trash can in the garage," I said. "Leave him alone unless he becomes a nuisance."

"What do you want to explore next?" she asked.

"I'd like to follow the creek up that ridge over there," I said. "See where it originates."

"How far does our property go?"

"Not to the beginning of the creek," I said. "We'll be trespassing, I suppose."

"Any houses up there?"

"I don't see any roads or driveways," I said. "No chimney smoke or other signs of life."

"You are still a keen observer," she said. "No matter how relaxed you tell me you are."

"Natural instinct," I said. "I'm just curious about our new surroundings."

My sleep that night was deep and restful, as it had been for weeks. Any dreams I remembered had been peaceful. I fought no demons overnight. Old loves and villains failed to appear. I was waking well before Brody each morning. I'd take my coffee down to the creek to wait patiently for a trout to show. Brody had given me that time as my own. She'd yell for me when breakfast was ready. We continued spending our days hiking and sightseeing. I was feeling fit and strong. I wasn't necessarily in fighting shape, but I didn't have to be. I had no enemies in the mountains of North Carolina. I had no friends either, other than Brody. As long as we enjoyed each other, that was all I needed. Cabin living was even better than we'd hoped.

Just as fall approached, we remembered to call the broker. We picked up a disposable phone, bought some minutes, and called him.

"Perfect timing," said Greg. "I've got a buyer wanting to line up a sea trial and survey. Any way you can come down here and drive the boat? Answer the guy's questions?"

"I hadn't really planned on it," I said. "Can you get a captain to help you out?"

"My guys are afraid to drive the thing," he said. "Single screw with no bow thruster. How'd you manage all these years?"

"I didn't dock it a whole lot for one thing," I said. "But you get a feel for how she handles after a while."

"Exactly," he said. "I'm asking you to handle it for the sea trial. Maybe give the new owner some pointers."

"Okay," I said. "We'll be there in a couple of days."

"I'll set it up," he said. "We'll get it all done in one day if the survey goes well."

I had my doubts about the survey. Surveyors are notoriously tough on old boats. *Leap of Faith* was not only old, she'd been run hard most of her life. She was sound, I made sure of that, but she had old boat idiosyncrasies that a novice buyer wouldn't understand. Maybe it was best if I were there to explain whatever faults the surveyor found. When she sold and how much she sold for really didn't make a lot of difference to me, but I'd go down there and see her through the process. I could say my final goodbyes to her. She deserved that much.

On the other hand, leaving the security of our cabin hideaway was going to be a pain in the ass. I wanted to leave immediately, get it over with, and return back home as soon as possible. We could stay on the boat until the paperwork was complete.

"It's going to be hard sleeping on her again," said Brody. "I love my big bed."

"For old-time's sake," I said. "One last fling."

"I understand," she said. "We gotta do what we gotta do."

We left the next morning and drove straight through. It was ten at night when we arrived. Inside the cabin was a package for Brody, addressed to the marina. She opened the box and pulled out a strange looking phone. There was also a note from Captain Fred. It explained the capabilities of the phone. It was a high-tech satellite phone that encrypted all communications. It could also piggyback on any wireless carrier's signal. Wherever you went you had access to Wi-Fi. He advised using the sat side for voice but assured us that it could not be hacked or surveilled.

Please call,

Fred Ford

It was late and we were tired from the road, but our curiosity got the better of us. Fred's number was pre-programmed.

"How's dirt dwelling treating you?" asked Fred.

"Quite well, thank you," I said. "Thanks for the phone, I guess."

"You're all healed up by now I presume?"

"Pretty much," I said. "Ninety percent or better."

"Good news," he said. "I've got a little favor to ask."

"No," said Brody. "Whatever it is the answer is no."

"I can assure you there will be nothing dangerous about it," he said. "It's a simple yacht delivery."

"Whose yacht?" I asked.

"Mine," he answered.

"Yours?"

"She turned up in Mexico. I hired a team of special operators to get her back. The Federales have some of the crew in custody, but the head of the organization was not aboard. It's under armed guard round the clock until I can pull it out of there."

"So hire a captain and fly him down there," I suggested.

"That's what I'm trying to do," he said. "This is your job, son. You know her. No one alive knows her like you do. My men will come along for the trip. Nothing bad will happen. They'll see to your safety."

Brody was shaking her head no, but I saw something in her eyes. Just a little bit of sparkle showed me that she could be convinced. Maybe a small thirst for adventure remained. I would have agreed immediately, but I couldn't make the decision by myself. Brody had to agree as well.

"Where's the boat exactly?" I asked Fred.

"Isla Mujeres," he said. "Tourist area. Big marina there with lots of Americans."

"You ever been to Isla Mujeres, Brody?" I asked.

"No, but it's not like we'd be going to hang out at a resort," she said. "In and out real quick."

"Fred's boat is better than any resort," I reminded her. "We'll be back in Florida in two days."

"You can take the boy out of the boat, but you can't take the boat out of the boy," she said. "I'd ask that you promise this will be the last time, but that's not likely."

"So you'll do it?" asked Fred.

"Do you really want to do this, Breeze," asked Brody.

"Only if you agree," I said. "Just say the word and we'll decline."

"Alright, damn it," she said. "Looks like we're going to Mexico."

Fourteen

First, we had an appointment to sell the boat. The buyer was nice enough and he seemed eager. His surveyor, on the other hand, was a pain in the ass. He made it his life's mission to point out every defect in detail, both big and small. There were some cracks in the countertop veneer. One window had some water damage around it. The floor in the forward cabins was squeaky. The twelve-volt wiring was less than professional. The plumbing was horrible. The bilge wasn't spotless, or even close. It was tough to listen to some stranger, who had never set foot on my boat before, tear it down. I took pleasure in the fact that he missed a few things that I knew about. I'd tell the buyer later after the boat was his.

The purchaser wanted to know three things. Is the hull sound? Does the engine run strong? Do all of the systems work? The answer to all three was yes. We took her out for a sea trial. I couldn't help but dwell on the fact that this would likely be the last time I'd ever pilot *Miss Leap*. I explained how I exited the slip. The boat pulled to starboard when in reverse. I let it walk that way on purpose to line up the next move. I left the wheel over hard to port. As soon as I put it in forward I goosed the throttle, making her turn faster. I did the same again in reverse, further straightening her out in the fairway. On the third turn, we were lined up and pointing outward. The buyer seemed to understand.

My broker, the buyer, the surveyor and I took a ride south on the ICW towards Boca Grande. Brody stayed behind at the pool. I kept her at a comfortable six knots until we cleared the swing bridge onto Gasparilla Island. The surveyor asked me to run it up to full throttle for a few minutes. I had rarely done so since I'd owned her. It didn't give me much more speed but it burned a lot more fuel. I eased her up to max rpm and studied the temperature gauge. It held steady at normal operating temperature. We managed eight knots in the calm waters of Gasparilla Sound. *Miss Leap* wondered what the hell I was doing pushing her so hard. After ten minutes I eased back on the throttle. The surveyor came back to the bridge and reported no problems or undue vibrations.

I let the buyer take the wheel for a while. He was smiling like a kid with a new toy. The surveyor seemed disappointed that he hadn't killed the deal with all of his nit-picking. He told the buyer that he'd have a full report complete with photos completed within a few days.

"I want this boat," said the buyer. "I'll need your report for the insurance company, but I think we've got a deal."

"Excellent," I said. "Greg will walk us through the paperwork."

Again I explained what I was doing as we returned to the slip. It was a left-hand turn into the dock. I slowed to a crawl just outside then goosed the throttle with the rudder hard to port. She spun almost all the way in. I used reverse, without moving the rudder to push the ass-end more to starboard. When we were perfectly lined up with the slip, I put her in gear for a few seconds and glided gently in.

"Good job, captain," said the buyer. "I see what you're doing there. I think I get it."

"You'll get the hang of it," I said. "I didn't know squat when I bought her."

We drove to Greg's office in Punta Gorda to complete the settlement transaction. I gathered the vessel's documentation, along with the title to the dinghy. Greg's wife handled all the transfers. After signing the necessary paperwork, I was handed a certified check for the amount we'd agreed upon. The deal was done. *Leap of Faith* now belonged to someone else. We all shook hands before leaving. Greg and his people had made it simple and painless. I drove back to the marina to say my final goodbye.

Brody was still at the pool. I rounded up the last of our belongings and loaded them in the car. I stood alone in the salon and looked around. The memories overwhelmed me. First I ran small batches of weed to town to sell to suburban housewives. Later I'd picked up bales from shrimpers in the Tortugas. I once loaded her down with a ton of cocaine from Columbia. I'd smuggled sweet Yolanda into the country from Cuba. I'd shared her with Holly as we traipsed around the Bahamas searching for something that we never quite found. I'd used her to hunt for gold off Cayo Costa. I'd helped Tommy recover his stash down in the Keys. I'd taken her all the way to South America, where Tommy and Holly together brought up tons of treasure with my help. I'd lost track of all the Caribbean islands she'd been to, but her home was in Pelican Bay. I'd likely never see that place again.

I thought of all the sunsets I'd watched from her deck, and the beaches she'd taken me to. I tried to recall all of the people I'd met in my travels. I guessed I'd never see One-Legged Beth, Diver Dan or Robin again. I had no idea where Holly was these days. I'd had some great adventures on that old boat, some bad ones too. She'd taken me everywhere a slow trawler could go in this world. She'd never let me down. I'd done my best to take good care of her. I'd patched her bullet holes, varnished her teak, and maintained her as best I was able. Our love affair was never breached, at least not until Brody came into my life. Giving up *Miss Leap* would never have been possible without Brody. I would have died aboard her in some deserted cove, old and lonely. She would have rotted away with neglect after my death. At least now she had a chance at a new life, just like me.

I went up on the bridge one last time and stood behind the wheel. I recalled all the times that dolphins had played in her bow wake. I couldn't count the hours that I'd sat at her helm. I'd lost track of the miles we'd covered.

You're a good girl, Miss Leap. A finer friend no man has ever had. You take care of the new guy just like you did me, hear?

I couldn't help myself. The tears welled up in my eyes. I just stood there and let them run down my cheeks. This part of my life was really over. *Miss Leap* had been the biggest part of it.

I'm sorry for any bad thing I ever said about you, especially during that poop thing. Now you go and have a happy life. Love you girl.

I climbed down the ladder and stepped onto the dock. I walked towards the pool without looking back. I made Brody go get the car so I wouldn't have to look at *Leap* again. I pictured myself sitting by the creek back at the cabin. A whole new world awaited me. Brody and I were moving on, but first, we had one last mission to run.

Fort Lauderdale was less than four hours away. We could get a room and check for flights to Mexico once we got there. My sadness kept me pretty quiet during the drive. It would have been better to get back to the cabin right away, but we had a job to do. Brody called Captain Fred and he booked our room and our flights for us. He was making it as easy as possible for us to do the job. All I had to do was drive a fancy yacht from Mexico to Florida. How hard could it be?

To get to Isla Mujeres we flew into Cancun. Fred had pre-booked a shuttle for us to get to the marina. The ride was less than an hour. We found his boat surrounded by heavily armed men. These were not amateur security guards. They looked like a team of Navy

SEALs. I was confronted long before I got close to the boat. Captain Fred appeared on deck and waved them off.

"Welcome to Mexico, kids," he said.

"Thanks for the ride," I said. "These guys look like they mean business."

"All tough operators," he said. "This detail is like a vacation for them."

"How many are there?"

"Eight," he said. "They rotate on and off duty. Two are on break."

"Have you found anything wrong with the boat?"

"Everything is in place," he said. "I had a team in here to sweep for listening devices and trackers. It is clean."

"What's our destination?"

"Lauderdale," he said. "Bahia Mar Marina. I'll pretend I'm Travis McGee."

"This boat ain't no *Busted Flush*," I said.

"Then I'll pretend Travis is my neighbor," he said. "Try to keep up with the pretty women coming and going."

"Are we fueled up and otherwise ready to go?"

"Just waiting on your arrival," he said. "I want to introduce you to the rest of the team before we shove off."

Fred rounded up our team of mercenaries on the back deck. They were all ex-military. Some were indeed SEALs. The rest were either Army Special Forces or the Marine version, MARSOCs. I wouldn't remember all their names, but Hank was the leader. He'd commanded SEAL teams in both Iraq and Afghanistan. They were all big guys but Hank was the biggest. They wore military-style uniforms with no insignia or indication of rank. They carried sophisticated looking weapons. You'd never get away with a show of force like this in an American marina. "Breeze and his gal Brody will be in command of this vessel," Fred began. "Your primary duty will be to ensure their safety. The safety of the ship is your secondary concern. Any actions that need to be taken to defend both the ship and its captain are up to Hank. Any decisions regarding navigation will be the responsibility of Breeze. He drives, you shoot. Understood?"

The men all nodded in agreement. Fred looked tiny standing in front of eight large men who were no strangers to violence, but he wasn't intimidated. He was the ultimate boss of this project, not me and not Hank. I felt like I should speak, show them that I wasn't intimidated either.

"We'll be taking an indirect route once we near Florida waters," I said. "I want to stay well offshore until we can get a direct bearing on Lauderdale. The boat's maximum speed is thirty-five knots, but we'll be running at twenty-five. Don't ask me to exceed the boat's capabilities. She won't run fifty and she won't zig-zag at speed. She won't stop bullets either."

"What's the probability of an attack?" asked Hank. "Not every day a yacht like this one gets shot at."

"Fred's last boat was shot up in the Bahamas. Later it was torched," I told them. "My own vessel has suffered bullet wounds in the past. Let's just say we have a history. Anything could happen, or nothing at all."

"Short of a missile or torpedo, we've got you covered," said Hank. "We can handle most any amount of small arms fire."

"Be wary of other vessels approaching too closely," I said. "Even aircraft."

"In the event of a hazard, you'll have eight shooters with plenty of ammo on station within seconds," said Hank.

"Until a hazard presents itself, let's enjoy the ride," said Fred.

I made a quick inspection of the engine rooms. Fluid levels were good. I laid in a course and prepared to leave the marina. The engines sounded good. All systems were operational. Brody supervised the lines, giving orders like she was one of the guys. I saw her handgun holstered at her hip. It gave me some comfort, in spite of all the firepower that our team carried. We eased out of the slip and began our journey. I patted the console of Fred's yacht.

"Come on, girl," I said. "We're just going for a little ride."

Isla Mujeres was on the far southeastern tip of Mexico. The closest landmass to our east was

Cuba. The plan was to travel on an arc halfway between Havana and the Keys, then make another arc out around Miami and up the east coast of Florida. Once the boat was safely tied up at Bahia Mar, we'd get a ride to the airport and pick up our car. If no obstacles appeared, we'd be ready to leave for North Carolina in a few days. I tried to summon my gut feelings on whether or not we'd have trouble. I got nothing. My gut was off duty, apparently. Maybe my time in the mountains had dulled that sixth sense. It didn't matter. It would all be over soon.

Once we hit open water, Hank's men set up big guns fore and aft. They were belt-fed monsters like you see in the movies. Hank came up to the bridge.

"Neither gunner has a three-sixty sweep," he said. "You may have to turn into the target if we are engaged."

"Did you bring shoulder-fired rockets too?"

"We have one," he said. "Old school. Not heat seeking. Let's hope we don't need it."

Fred and Brody joined me on the bridge. We made small talk to pass the time, but I was curious about something.

"Let's drill down into who might be giving you all this grief," I said to Fred.

"The possibilities are many," he said. "I've given it a lot of thought, but I don't have an answer for you."

"You've done business all over the world," I said. "Including plenty of places that are politically unstable. Lately, you've been to Columbia, but I know you did some deals in Lagos and the Philippines."

"The biggest shithole I've ever dealt with was Florida politics," he said. "The D.C. swamp is a mud hole compared to Florida."

"But you built your airport," I said. "Swamp successfully navigated."

"Not without stepping on some toes," he said.

"You pissed off some power brokers," I said.

"Snookered them," he said. "Outmaneuvered and just plain ripped them off."

"It's a dog-eat-dog world," I said.

"And that land where the airport sits has been pissed on by every swinging dick from Tallahassee to Miami, including me."

"So which one of those enemies is most likely to mount a campaign to make your life miserable?"

"The sugar baron brothers," he said. "If I had to guess, but they don't seem like the violent type to me."

"Remember, so far there's been no violence," I said. "They could have shot up your boat down in St. Croix. They had you in custody but didn't harm you. *Incognito* was blown up but no one was aboard."

"Now I've gone and stolen my boat back from them," he said.

"How do you think they'll respond?"

"Maybe they'll run out of patience with the non-violent approach," he said.

We went on to discuss other potential enemies. We talked about government actors in Columbia and the Philippines. Fred had caused a big stink in the Philippines, but that had been many years ago, decades even. Columbian officials were all deeply influenced by the drug cartels, but Fred had been careful not to cross them. Besides, drug cartels would shoot first and ask questions later. The other option was one of the big tech companies that he'd beaten in a race to develop some new software. What if Google wanted to mess with you? Their reach extended around the globe and their resources were virtually unlimited. Silicon Valley geeks didn't seem to be the type to resort to violence either.

Fred was non-committal. He couldn't be certain if it was any of them. We went over some other outlying possibilities, but none of them had the resources that had been brought to bear in his case. The surveillance tools and global movement capability pointed to a sophisticated group with lots of money and connections. Not many people on earth had the type of connections and influence possessed by the sugar barons. They were the most likely suspects in my mind, but we had no proof. We couldn't be sure.

I adjusted course to keep our distance from Cuban waters. I'd had more than one run-in with the Cuban military and I didn't want any repeats. Of course, I hadn't been escorted by a group of military bad-asses back then. If a Cuban gunboat approached us, they'd be in for a big surprise. We saw nothing out of the ordinary until we reached a point mid-way between Marathon and Havana.

"Chopper approaching from the south," yelled Hank. "Low and fast."

I had the urge to yell "Battle Stations," but the men were already positioned. The helicopter was on us in no time. It buzzed over our bow and made a sharp turn to starboard, circling around for another pass. It was not military or Coast Guard. It had a corporate look to it. It had no business passing over us so closely. I couldn't think of a reason for it to be out there at all. It had come from the south. That could only mean Cuba. The sugar barons were Cubans. We were forty-five miles north of Havana in international waters, well within the range of a corporate chopper.

We were getting close to solving our mystery. What were their intentions? We found out on their second pass. The craft turned broadside to us and the side door was flung open. A machine gun opened fire on our starboard side, strafing us from bow to stern. Our mercenaries returned fire with a vengeance. The chopper quickly veered off and flew out of range. The whole thing lasted a few seconds.

"Is anybody hurt?" I yelled.

"All accounted for," came the reply.

Where was Brody? Should I speed up or take evasive action? I couldn't outrun the chopper so I held steady and maintained speed. I kept eye contact with the enemy. When it circled back around I took cover as best I could. Our men didn't wait to be fired upon first. The big guns opened up even before their target was in range, discouraging our enemy from getting too close. They zoomed by us and fired off a quick barrage that hit nothing. They were traveling too fast to be accurate.

Hank showed up on the bridge. He knew a little something about helicopters.

"That's an Airbus ACH160," he said. "A twenty million dollar machine. Cruising speed about one-fifty. Governments and Fortune 500 CEO's buy them. You've got some wealthy enemies."

"Not me, Fred," I said. "I just work here."

"We can't outrun them," he said. "We can hold them off like we just did, but we'll eventually run out of ammo. If they're smart they'll toy with us until we can't shoot back."

"Can you take it out with your missile?"

"Not at that speed," he said. "It'd be pure luck to hit it."

"Can we decoy them into thinking we're low on ammo?" I asked. "Trick them into turning broadside like the first time, then hit them with the rocket."

"If we had some decent cover," he said. "If we let them hover, my men will be easy targets."

"What kind of range does that thing have?" I asked.

"Five hundred miles at cruise," he said. "But they've been pushing it hard. Three hundred maybe."

We were only fifty miles or so from Cuba, which I assumed was their starting point. They could fly around out here for hours and still make it back on fuel. I decided to change course. I wanted to run northeast towards the open Atlantic, put some distance between us and their home base. I pushed the throttles to the max. The big Hatteras responded. The further the chopper had to travel the sooner they'd get low on fuel. I doubted they would shoot at us if we were close to Miami. I started hailing the Coast Guard over the radio. When they responded I reported being fired upon by a helicopter in international waters. I gave them our position, course bearing, and speed. They advised me to make haste towards Miami. A gunship would be dispatched to the area.

I guess the Coast Guard doesn't equip their rescue choppers with machine guns. They'd be a sitting duck against the faster Airbus anyway. We all braced for the next attack. The chopper did a fast flyby without shooting. Our men wasted a few hundred rounds from the big guns. I thought I heard bullets bouncing off metal, but no damage was apparent. The next time the chopper fired on us again. It flew a little slower and the gunner was on target. Fred's boat took heavy damage. The chopper was clearly hit but didn't seem affected. I didn't like how this was going.

Brody came up just as the Miami skyline came into view. I wondered if she wanted to be together when we died.

"One last adventure," she said. "What could go wrong?"

I had no time to respond as the chopper was on us again. I shielded Brody with my body as the windows of the pilothouse were blown out. The gunfire lasted longer this time. I snuck a glance up and saw that the chopper hadn't flown straight past us. It made a tight circle and resumed firing before running away. The bow gunner was down. Brody and I were unhurt, other than some scratches from the shattered glass.

"Two men hit," yelled Hank. "We've got enough ammo left for one more pass."

I pointed at the tall buildings of Miami. At our speed, we were closing in fast. The chopper didn't have much time left unless he wanted to chase us right into the harbor. I hailed the Coast Guard again.

"Gunship is in the outbound channel now," came the reply.

I wished we had more speed. I wished we had more ammo. I wished I was sitting by the creek back at the cabin. I wished that Brody was safe in North Carolina, not getting shot at off the coast of Miami. Wishing did me no good. The chopper set up for another approach. I saw Hank on one knee, holding a rocket launcher on his shoulder.

"Clear back-blast area," he yelled.

Just as the chopper started to turn to allow their gunner to fire, Hank let loose the rocket. Had he hit his target it would have been something to see. Hitting a moving target while on a moving ship proved too much to ask. The rocket screamed past the chopper just above the rotor.

"Fuck," said Hank.

I don't know if it was the rocket or our proximity to the city that deterred further attacks, but the chopper flew south at a high rate of speed. When I turned my eyes forward, I saw the Coast Guard gunship approaching. Maybe that was it.

"Captain, continue your course and speed," came the voice on the radio. "We'll stay on station until you're safely in port."

"You saw the chopper, right?" I asked.

"Target identified," he said. "No point in pursuit, but we'll protect the port until we're recalled."

"Thanks," I said. "But we don't have a slip in Miami. We were bound for Fort Lauderdale."

"Proceed directly to the Coast Guard station," he instructed. "Someone will be waiting to debrief you and your crew."

Fifteen

I was concerned about our casualties. We'd taken heavy fire and I knew that at least one man had been hit. Fred's boat was heavily damaged. Our joyride had turned into a nightmare. We'd have plenty of questions to answer once we tied up at the Coast Guard Station. I should have known better, but that's the way it went with me. Sometimes good intentions turned into SNAFUs. Brody stuck her head in the door to let me know that she was okay.

"We've got two gunshot wounds down there," she said. "One of them looks bad. I've already called for ambulances to meet us, but don't waste any time getting us docked."

"Glad to see that you're not hurt," I said.

"Likewise," she said. "But we're about to encounter a major cluster you know."

"Talk to Fred," I said. "Let's put him in charge of our diplomacy. They'll have investigators all over us."

"I'm on it," she said.

I concentrated on navigating the busy harbor with as much speed as I could manage without throwing a dangerous wake. The Coast Guard had sent out a radio message urging mariners to give us a wide berth. I made out the flags and vessels of their station and steered towards it. I slowed considerably as I passed their break wall. I saw a bunch of Coasties waving me toward an open spot, probably vacated by the gunboat. I carefully maneuvered close enough for lines to be tossed. I heard Brody down below giving out instructions. I shut the engines down without allowing them to cool down like I normally would. I had to get below to assist and assess the damage.

Our two gunshot victims had been bandaged up. All the men had been wearing flak jackets and helmets, but bullets had found their legs. The bow gunner was bleeding profusely in spite of his bandages. His skin was white and he was not alert. The second victim was in less danger, but his knee was probably wrecked for life. I felt horrible for their suffering. They'd made it through multiple tours in the Middle East only to get shot up here. I couldn't accept fault though. Fred had hired them and they'd signed on voluntarily. Still, I was the captain of the ship. I was at least partially responsible.

We all worked together to transfer the wounded to the waiting ambulances. Hank rode with the more severely injured man. Coast Guard personnel escorted the ambulances away from the dock and to the hospital. The rest of us were milling around alongside our battered boat when we were confronted by the station commander.

"This vessel and its crew will be restricted to this base until investigators allow you to leave," he said. "I've got some available bunks inside, but we can't provide the kind of accommodations you may be accustomed to."

"On whose authority?" asked Captain Fred. "We've committed no crimes."

"Mine," the commander replied. "I can't be sure of that. You didn't get shot up for no reason at all."

Fred started to speak again but I interrupted him. There was no point in arguing. We had nothing to hide.

"Look," I began. "We're all pretty beat up and we've suffered through an ordeal today. Send in your investigators when they arrive. In the meantime, let us get cleaned up and catch some rest. We can deal with all of this later."

"Those of you who choose to stay aboard are welcome to do so," said the commander. "But I'll have men on guard for the duration of your stay. If you choose to accept my invitation to stay with us, you'll be free to move around inside the barracks."

The remainder of Hank's men chose to go inside. Brody, Fred and I stayed on the boat. We were prisoners on our own vessel.

"I'm starting to think you're bad luck, Breeze," Fred said. "Half the times you drive one of my boats, it gets shot all to hell."

"I have a slightly different perspective," I replied. "Half the times I drive your boat, I get shot at. Maybe it's you who's bad luck."

"Probably so," he admitted. "Looks like I pissed off the wrong people this time."

"Assuming it's the sugar baron brothers out to get you," I said. "Why are they so mad? What did you do to piss them off exactly?"

"Long story," he began. "But the only way I could get that land to build the airport was to cohort with them. It's smack dab in the middle of sugar country, plus they had the political pull to help get the approvals. At first, they owned forty-nine percent of the company. We had a contingency that stated one of us had to buy the other out once we reached a certain stage in the process. I had everything I owned invested in it. It could go wrong and never get permitted. I could get bought out by the sugar boys, or I could come out with one-hundred percent ownership."

"How did that translate into making you billions?" I asked.

"That's the part they didn't know about," he said. "I had secretly negotiated with the Port of Miami. When the contractual deadline approached, I made them think the deal was going sour. They were happy to let me buy them out."

"But it wasn't going sour," I said.

"I may have misrepresented the truth," he said. "Still, they didn't realize just how bad I'd bamboozled them until I sold the whole kit and caboodle to the Port Authority."

"They missed the chance to make billions," I said. "They felt cheated."

"The fact that I'd acted in bad faith added to the sting," he said. "But it's a dog-eat-dog world. They'd have done the same if they would have spotted the opportunity."

"Now you've lost one boat and this one is in rough shape," I said. "The insurance company is going to be awfully suspicious."

"I can't make a claim for this," he said. "They already paid out on the first claim when it was stolen."

"So technically the insurance company owns the boat now," I said.

"In the shape it's in they can have it," he said. "It's not so much that I was in love with the thing in the first place. It was the stealing it back that mattered to me. Show them I wouldn't lay down for them."

"We catch bullets as a result," I said. "Two of those guys you hired are hurt pretty badly. It could have been me or Brody."

"Consequences of rash decisions," he said. "I'll take care of those guys. You too, if you need it."

"Right now we need you to concentrate on whatever kind of investigation is about to take place," I said. "We're innocent but it looks bad."

"I'll tell them the truth," he said. "Maybe it will lead to catching whoever shot us up. Eventually get back to the power behind it."

"If the chopper is in Cuba I'm afraid there isn't much they can do," I said.

"Always the pessimist," he said.

"Hope for the best but prepare for the worst," I said.

"I know, I know," he said. "People suck and life ain't fair."

"Exactly."

I felt as if I'd been the one giving the advice. Normally, Fred was the more wise and worldly one. He lived on the right side of the law. He called me when he needed someone who wasn't afraid to live on the wrong side of it. His generosity made me happy to oblige. We'd become friends. It wasn't just business for us anymore. I'd helped him with a family affair. He'd helped me with some legal ones. I'd managed the movement of his boats because he trusted me. I'd proven that I could be counted on. So had Brody. Now it looked like our association would soon end. That saddened me a bit, but I hadn't lost sight of our dream to live in the mountains. I'd gotten a taste of it, and it agreed with me. Brody had come on this trip reluctantly. When this was over, we'd return to our happily ever after. I'd never ask her to join this kind of mission again.

We scrounged up a meal from our meager provisions and sat down together to eat.

"What's going to happen next?" asked Brody.

"They'll search the boat and grill all of us," said Fred. "They won't find anything. That'll frustrate them. We'll be guilty until proven innocent in their eyes."

"What about our mercenaries?" she asked. "Those weapons aren't exactly for civilian use."

"We were in international waters," said Fred. "We were driven into U.S. territory by the chopper."

"That won't stick," she said. "What would our destination be if not the States? The Bahamas would frown on those guns even more."

"I may have to pull some strings," he said. "Maybe call in a few favors."

"I'm guessing that your enemies can pull more strings and call in more favors than you," I said. "That's why we're in this mess."

"Even if we could prove they were behind the attack, do you think they'd ever be prosecuted?" I asked.

"We know enough about our two-tiered justice system to answer that," said Brody.

We were about to be under intense scrutiny. Our arrest wasn't out of the question, even though we'd been the victims. Brody and I both were widely known by the FBI and even some Washington insiders. Our current predicament would smell like dead fish to them. Yet, we weren't running drugs or trafficking humans. We were clear, other than the firearms violations. Our only defense had to be the truth. Fred needed to explain exactly what was going on and let the chips fall where they may.

Two agents from the Coast Guard Investigative Service showed up the next morning. I didn't know such an agency existed. I thought maybe NCIS would handle it. The active duty member of the duo was Chief Warrant Officer Brewer. His civilian counterpart was Agent Hanson. I didn't quite understand the makeup of the CGIS, but there they were onboard Fred's boat.

"We intend to fully cooperate," said Fred. "But please advise me as to your jurisdiction in this case before we get started."

"Nice to meet you, Mr. Ford," said Brewer. "I am charged with investigating violations related to or within the maritime jurisdiction of the United States. I'd say that automatic weapons fire within the EEZ qualifies."

"Just so you know," said Fred. "The automatic weapons fire was directed at us and began outside the twenty-mile line. Our men only returned fire in self-defense. We weren't much concerned with whether or not we'd crossed that line."

"The question is why you came under attack in the first place," said Brewer.

"Clearly I have enemies who wanted to kill me," said Fred. "But not because of any crime that I've committed."

"I understand you're a rich and powerful man, Mr. Ford," he said. "That's earned you rich and powerful enemies?"

"Something like that" Fred answered.

"Would you care to elaborate on that?" asked Brewer.

"We'll get to all of that later," said Fred. "Why don't you go ahead and conduct your search. After you find nothing maybe we can talk with a lower level of suspicion on your part."

"You do realize that the Coast Guard lives to conduct searches on vessels?"

"Be our guest," said Fred. "Bring on the hounds."

"That is being arranged as we speak," said Brewer.

He was not a casual man. He took his duties seriously. His partner hadn't spoken, but had observed the three of us closely. Probably looking for signs of deception. The two of them went outside to wait for the search team. "Do we need lawyers?" I asked. "Not yet," said Fred. "But if they put us in a cell or holding room, don't speak until you get one. If they let me make some calls, I'll get us outside help. Right now we've got some wiggle room, but if they take us in, demand a lawyer and don't talk until you get one."

Six Coasties and a dog arrived. We were asked to step off the boat. I stood and watched for a few minutes. They pried bullets out of fiberglass. Those had come from the chopper. They also bagged shell casings they found on the deck. Those had come from our guys. They inspected the big guns that were still installed on tripods both fore and aft. They carefully unloaded them and took them into evidence. We were eventually escorted indoors and offered cheeseburgers from the mess hall.

Hank had returned from the hospital and was inside with the rest of his men. The bow gunner was in serious condition. He'd lost a lot of blood but the artery had been patched up. He'd most likely be okay. The other guy needed a new knee but was in stable condition. I was relieved to learn that they would both survive. I didn't need another death on my conscience.

"I hope your boat is clean," said Hank. "That Warrant Officer has a stick up his ass."

"There is nothing for them to find," said Fred. "Our only real concern is the weapons."

"In third world countries we just shoot our way out," Hank said. "But here we'll have to deal with the bullshit."

"You're still on my dime," Fred said. "I'll hire lawyers and do whatever it takes to protect all of you."

"You still glad you hired us?"

"We'd all be dead without you," Fred said.

"They certainly tried hard enough," said Hank. "I'm curious as to why that is."

"They've been coming at me and coming at me," Fred said. "Each time it has escalated to another level. I'm afraid they won't quit until they finish the job."

"That's because you've been playing defense," Hank said. "You've got to take the fight to them. Stop sitting around waiting for the next attack. Strike them first."

"I don't know how to do that," Fred said.

"You get us out of this mess and we'll sit down and come up with a plan," Hank offered. "My team is much happier on offense."

"Any ideas, Breeze?" asked Fred.

"Let me think it over," I said. "I like the idea though."

"I do not like the idea," said Brody.

"It's not really even an idea yet," I said. "Let's withhold judgment until a plan takes shape."

"We can't fight twenty-million dollar helicopters and machine guns, Breeze," she said. "Don't be foolish."

I wasn't thinking along those lines. I was thinking about a way to hurt those sugar barons. The first inkling of an idea was starting to form in my mind, but I kept it to myself. There were many details to be worked out.

Sixteen

The search lasted for several hours. Finally, Chief Warrant Officer Brewer informed us that they found nothing. There was no evidence whatsoever that we'd been hauling drugs or participating in any illegal activity. He was still curious about all the weaponry and advised that we could all tell our story the next day.

"Please, take advantage of whatever hospitality we have to offer," he said. "We'll discuss this further tomorrow."

"May we return to our vessel now?" asked Fred.

"Of course," he said. "Just bear with me and remain on the premises."

Brewer was slightly less antagonistic, but we were still prisoners. We went back to the boat and Fred retired to his stateroom to make some phone calls. Brody and I hoped that his connections would pay off for us. We didn't want to stay in limbo for much longer. We lounged around in the salon waiting for Fred to tell us how it went. Two hours passed before he rejoined us.

"Our investigator friend will be receiving a series of messages from some key people in Washington," he said. "I predict he'll stand down, with apologies."

"Good news," I said. "Sure is nice to have friends in high places."

"I've pulled my last string up there on our behalf," he said. "You and I need to stay off their radar in the future."

"Brody and I intend to do just that," I said. "Once this situation is all cleared up."

"It will be over in the morning," Fred assured me. "We'll be free to go by lunchtime."

"I don't just mean being stuck here," I said. "You've got unfinished business with those sugar boys. You've got hired guns willing to help. Let's try and end this before Brody and I disappear forever."

"What are you talking about, Breeze?" asked Brody.

"I'm working on a plan," I told her. "I've got an idea but I need to do some research. It does not involve violence but it will send a strong message."

"I can't wait to hear this one," she said.

"Soon enough," I said. "I need some vital information, maps and such. I need to talk it over with Hank. I think it will work. You will too when I'm finished."

"I'll log you into my computer," said Fred. "Get whatever you need."

I spent the rest of the night searching the web for the information that I needed, with Brody's help. I printed out several copies of maps for the land just south of Lake O. I identified each lock along the Okeechobee Waterway. I located each flood control gate and canal along the southern edge of the dike. I looked up water flow gauges and historic lake levels. I took note of the population of the towns of Clewiston and Belle Glade. I was no engineer, but I was putting together a plan that we could execute, with the help of Hank's team. Brody figured out what the goal was. I didn't want Fred to know until after I consulted with Hank. His team was two men short after all.

We'd missed dinner and the galley was woefully low on supplies. Fred apologized for not cooking us a gourmet meal. He hadn't had the opportunity to restock the pantry down in Mexico. Hank's team had been hard on what we did have. We walked over to the mess hall trying to find some grub. Dinner service was over, but the cooks said they could whip up something in a few minutes.

We found the rest of Hank's team telling war stories to some Seamen and Petty Officers. They were all young kids and seemed enthralled by the grizzled veterans. The cooks brought us plates of spaghetti with some slightly stale bread. We bought drinks from a vending machine and listened to Taliban tales told in a non-politically correct manner. The soldiers had a serious dislike of ragheads, camel jockeys, and goat fuckers. This born out of the loss of some of their friends to IEDs and other cowardly tactics.

Some of their stories were disturbing, especially to Brody. I couldn't imagine going through what they'd experienced over there. They were strong, brave men who'd been hardened by the atrocities they'd witnessed. Polite society had little room for them. That's why they'd chosen to sell their services to whomever was willing to pay. Fred was writing the checks at the moment. I hoped they'd be onboard with what I was planning.

There was no sign of Brewer. He probably had a nice house in Coconut Grove. Maybe he ate dinner at that goat cheese place Brody and I had visited. He'd been respectful enough to Fred and Brody, but I sensed that he didn't hold me in the same regard. He likely resented the fact that I was under Fred's umbrella and he couldn't treat me like the trash he thought I was. Screw him, I thought. Soon he'd have to swallow his pride and watch us walk free, no matter how guilty he thought we were.

We went back to the boat and laughed at the fact that at least we were safe from Cuban helicopters with machine guns. We suspected that the Coast Guard gunship would have to remain at sea until we got Fred's boat out of its way.

"What happens when we go back out to sea?" I asked. "How do we know we won't be making ourselves a target again?"

"If we stay inside the three-mile line they won't dare try anything," said Brody.

"I'm sure the base commander will hear from Brewer," said Fred. "He'll probably offer us an escort to Lauderdale."

"That would be nice," I said. "Federal law enforcement would be working to protect me instead of trying to hunt me down. Nice change."

"What will you do with this thing once we get there?" Brody asked Fred.

"Alert the insurance company, I suppose," he answered. "Let them deal with it. I'll pay a month's rent and wash my hands of it."

"Such a shame," she said.

"Until this thing is over with the sugar barons," he said. "My boats are just an easy target. I'm tired of sacrificing them to my personal war."

"Let's see how tomorrow plays out," I said. "Maybe I can help settle the score once we get out of here."

We called it a night and went to bed. Sitting around doing nothing all day was just as tiring as a full day's work. I slept deeply, allowing the dreams to come. I was aboard *Leap of Faith* with Fred, Brody, and Hank's team. We were caught in a raging torrent which swept us over the Herbert Hoover Dike at the southern edge of Lake Okeechobee. We floated down the main street in the town of Clewiston. People were in the water everywhere. It was too deep for them to stand. We began rescuing everyone we could reach. The boat filled up with people and animals like Noah's Ark. One hundred people crammed the decks. Their weight threatened to capsize us, but still, we continued pulling more people aboard. The burden was too much. I realized that we were all going to die. I also realized that it was my fault.

Brody woke me from my nightmare. She was a veteran of dealing with my dreams. She was always patient and loving. She knew that I took them to heart.

"My plan needs a little more work," I said.

"Is that what you were dreaming about?"

"I got a vivid reminder of the risks involved," I told her. "I've got to figure out how to mitigate those risks."

"Maybe Hank can help," she said. "We'll talk to him tomorrow."

Morning arrived and brought with it high hopes for a successful resolution to our captivity. We met Brewer and his partner in the Station Commander's office. The commander was also present.

"Much has happened overnight," said Brewer. "But first I need a few questions answered."

Fred, Brody and I all exchanged glances. He wasn't going to let us walk out of there without getting what he wanted.

"We said we'd cooperate," said Fred. "What do you need to know?"

"Why did you have a team of heavily armed mercenaries aboard your vessel?" he asked.

"Because we thought there was a possibility that we'd come under attack," Fred said. "As you can see we were correct."

"Why is that?"

"I seem to be in an ever-escalating dispute with some actors of ill repute."

"Do you mind telling me who that is?" asked Brewer.

"We have our suspicions," said Fred. "But nothing that we can prove."

"What about the helicopter?"

"What about it?" asked Fred.

"Where did it come from and how did they know where you were?"

"It came from Cuba," I said. "No doubt about it. Not hard to keep an eye on the narrow stretch of water where they intercepted us."

"Hundred foot yachts are still a rare occurrence in the Florida Straits," said Fred.

"We have some information on the chopper," said Brewer. "Our gunboat crew was able to decipher the tail numbers."

"Who owns it?" asked Fred.

"We traced it through a series of Limited Liability Corporations and fronts," he said. "Eventually we pinned it to certain brothers who own a very influential business right here in the state of Florida."

"Big Sugar?" I asked.

"Precisely," he replied. "You may be aware that these brothers are Cuban dissidents. Pursuit of the chopper on Cuban soil or within Cuban airspace would likely create an international uproar. I've been advised to discontinue that part of the investigation. The CIA has been made aware."

"How can they use Cuba as a launch pad with impunity?" I asked.

"I'm more curious how they escaped that island with their wealth intact," said Fred.

"Friendly with the Castros, no doubt," said Brewer. "The State took their cane plantation but allowed them to retain the rest of their assets. Just speculation of course."

"Now they rule Florida politics and a good chunk of D.C. as well," Fred said.

"Not the type of enemy one would normally cultivate," said Brewer. "Plus it makes my job impossible."

"So there is no legal recourse?" asked Brody. "You're going to let them get away with trying to kill us?"

"The decision was not mine to make," he said. "I got a dozen phone calls last night and this morning. There were two camps. One told me that I should ignore any technical violations on your part and set you free immediately."

"What was the other camp telling you?" Fred asked.

"That I was to go nowhere near the sugar barons," he said. "They were strictly off-limits."

"Is the decision to let us go out of your hands as well?" I asked.

"Let's just say that my career is at stake," he said. "In the meantime, I've checked all of your backgrounds. I've been made aware of Miss Brody's tenuous relationship with the FBI. I've learned that Mr. Ford has some powerful friends as well as enemies. The only one with an actual criminal history is you, Mr. Breeze."

"Just Breeze is fine, thanks," I said.

"I wouldn't think that someone of Mr. Ford's stature would employ someone such as you," he said.

"My skills come in handy from time to time," I replied.

"He can handle a boat like nobody's business," said Fred.

"Your disdain for my lousy pedigree is showing, Brewer," I said.

"I'm not fond of drug dealers and tax evaders," he responded.

"Was I included in your orders to let us go free?" I asked.

"Unfortunately yes," he said. "You're not currently on anyone's wanted list. You're not on probation. I can't hold you."

I turned to Brody for support. She gave me a look that said *just let it go*. I decided to take her advice and quit while we were ahead. Our freedom was more important than setting this guy straight. I knew that my debt to society had been paid. I also knew that I'd recently spent several hundred thousand dollars delivering aid to hurricane victims. I didn't need Brewer's approval. Fred interjected.

"The fact that you won't pursue the bad guys means that they are free to come after me again," he said. "The least you can do is give us an escort to Lauderdale. We can be out of your hair in thirty minutes."

"We'll be taking Hank and his team with us," I said.

"You won't be taking the weapons," Brewer said.

"Then we'll definitely need the Coast Guard to ride shotgun," I replied.

We all looked at the commander. Brewer gave him a nod.

"I'll give you two fast boats with M-60s," said the commander. "I need to get that gunboat back in here."

"We'll take it," I said. "Much appreciated."

Chief Warrant Officer Brewer and his partner walked out of the room without saying another word. I went back to the boat to start the engines while Brody and Fred went to get the team. I didn't dawdle over the political lessons I learned that day. I just wanted to get the hell out of there and plan Fred's revenge.

Seventeen

The Coast Guard radio operator warned all vessels to stay clear as we made our exit with two fast boats on either side of us. Their bow-mounted machine guns looked menacing. The twenty-year-old Petty Officers did not. They did, however, remain at the ready for the entire trip. Fortunately, no helicopters swooped in to take shots at us. Our escorts veered off as we entered the channel into Fort Lauderdale. After we got tied up, Fred took the whole crew to Ruth's Chris Steakhouse.

After we got some food and drink in us, I was pressed to reveal my plan. I asked everyone to quiet down and motioned for them to lean in closely. I had their full attention. I whispered my intentions.

"We're going to flood the cane fields," I said. "Ruin the whole crop."

"Can we do that?" asked Hank.

"I've got some ideas," I said. "I'll bring you all up to speed but not here in public."

"Billy is our munitions guy," he said. "We'll need a few days to procure whatever you need."

"I'll turn my house into command central," said Fred. "I can accommodate all of you. It's secure and I've got all the technology you'll need for your research."

"We'll need to negotiate a new deal," said Hank. "This is a different mission than what we originally signed up for."

"Not a problem," said Fred.

"We won't be too hard on you," said Hank. "This sounds like something we can sink our teeth into. Get a little payback."

"We're going on the offense," I said. "Per your suggestion."

We all agreed to rendezvous at Fred's place in Central Florida in three days. Phone numbers and email addresses were exchanged. Hank would contact more members for his team and put them on standby. We wouldn't know how many men we needed until our plan was solidified. Fred called the caretaker of his property and asked him to arrange for delivery of plenty of food and drink. He also booked a hotel room for the man and his family. We needed extra beds for Hank's team.

Brody, Fred and I got a ride to the airport where we'd left our car. Hank's team dispersed as well. Everyone could get a few days to rest before we met again. During the drive to central Florida, Fred expressed his eagerness to send a message to the sugar barons. He also expressed doubts about my goal to flood the cane fields.

"You'll be in on the planning every step of the way," I assured him. "Brody and I will study the infrastructure thoroughly. Hank can help us with the logistics. We'll make it happen."

"You've got all those people living below the dike," Fred said.

"I'm well aware," I told him. "We'll take great pains to protect lives. I can't say the same for property though."

"Water always wins," he said. "But some of those places could use a good wash-down."

"Do the workers still live in shitty conditions?" I asked.

"Miserable," he said. "But no one cares. They're mostly migrants from the West Indies and Jamaica, with some Cubans thrown in the mix. A sugar man will tell you they have a natural ability for working the fields, an innate instinct. Truth is they're the only ones willing to work under those conditions, mostly due to fear of deportation."

"Guest workers?" asked Brody.

"Just another example of the sugar industry living off government largesse," he said. "Restrictions on imported sugar, and artificially propped up prices and cheap labor on work visas."

The sugar industry in America has never really operated in a free market. Cane sugar in Florida wouldn't exist if the state hadn't drained the Everglades. It would disappear if the Army Corps of Engineers didn't permanently alter the landscape and manage it at taxpayer's expense to expose the dirt and keep the water levels just right for growing. What remains of the Everglades wouldn't be starved for fresh water if the dike didn't exist. Both coasts would be spared the blue-green algae and nutrient laden water that's diverted from the lake. South Florida's environment is under constant attack by seemingly unstoppable forces, all centered around the preservation and protection of Big Sugar.

I thought we might be able to put a kink in that arrangement, at least temporarily. At a minimum, we could show certain sugar barons that Fred had the will and the ability to fight back. We got right to work as soon as we settled into Fred's house.

There were two components to controlling the water levels in the lake. Locks on the Caloosahatchee and St. Lucie rivers were the first. Flood control gates, or spillways, were the second. The three of us researched each component. We determined their locations, dimensions, potential rate of flow, and hours of operation. The locks did not operate at night. Clearly, our mission would take place in darkness.

We learned that over ninety percent of the lake was covered in thick green algae. Recent releases to both coasts had angered the citizenry and local politicians screamed for relief. Governor Scott toured the affected areas and declared a state of emergency for Lee County on the west coast and Martin County on the east coast. The Army Corps agreed to stop the releases for nine consecutive days. We were already two days into that pause. We now had a time constraint. We didn't want water flowing into the rivers. We wanted it to flow over the cane fields.

We didn't need to control all five locks in the system, just one on either side of the lake. I identified four major spillways that would most directly flood the fields. Using two-man teams, we'd need a total of twelve operators, including Brody and me. We notified Hank of the need for additional men and the timing issue. He said they were ready to go at a moment's notice. I asked them to come to our location as soon as possible. We'd need time to get whatever supplies he deemed necessary and to put our heads together on the best way to proceed. I wanted to secure the locks and their corresponding spillways in the closed position, while simultaneously opening the southern spillways. They couldn't be permanently disabled or the resulting flood would be catastrophic. We needed to temporarily make them inoperative, but not so badly that they couldn't be repaired and closed again in a timely fashion. We continued gathering as much information and data as we could while we waited for the team to arrive. We looked at pictures of the spillway gates, zooming in on the equipment that operated them. We printed everything that might be relevant.

Hank's team arrived the next day. After they unloaded all their gear, Hank sat down with us to go over the maps and pictures. I used a satellite photo of Lake Okeechobee and pointed out the various pieces of infrastructure.

"We want to keep these locks and associated gates closed," I said. "Moore Haven on the western side and the Mayaca Lock on the east."

"Are you looking to physically deter someone from opening them, or to disable them in the closed position?"

"Break them," I said. "Jam them up but not so they can't be fixed easily. We're counting on the Army Corps of Engineers to respond and divert the water so people below the dike don't die."

I pointed out the towns of Clewiston and Belle Glade on the map. Clewiston was on the southwest corner of the lake between two tracts of land owned by a different sugar corporation. Belle Glade east of center near the Hillsboro Canal. The target area was dead center, just south of the dike and between the two towns. That's where we wanted the most water. I pointed out the spillways.

"We want these to be jammed in the open position," I said. "Again, not permanently disabled."

"The Corps will show up and shut them down," Hank said. "At least you hope so."

"That should be their first priority," I said. "They won't get to the locks until later, once they realize the extent of the flood."

"How do we know they'll get things under control before it's too late?" he asked. "You're putting a lot of faith in a bunch of engineers."

"First of all, it's their job," I said. "All of this stuff is in case of a hurricane. They manipulate these gates all the time."

"But?"

"But I think the teams will have to stay on station in case they don't arrive quickly enough," I said.

"How will we know what's going on downstream?"

"Fred will stay here and monitor water levels," I said. "Each canal has a variety of gauges that show current depth."

"How deep should we allow it to get?"

"Three feet above the canal banks should do it," I said. "The fields will be inundated. The towns will have a foot or so of water in them. An inconvenience but not the end of the world."

"So we jam the spillway gates open," he said. "We sit and wait for the Corps to show up. If they come to the rescue, we split. If the water gets too high before they arrive, we close the gates on Fred's signal."

"That's pretty much it," I said. "Two of your guys will keep the St. Port Mayaca closed. Brody and I will handle the Moore Haven Lock. The rest work the spillways."

"We've got comms for everybody," he said. "We need to work out deployment and exfiltration."

I pointed out each location on the map. Moore Haven was the far western edge of our operating territory. Moving eastward I came to the Miami Canal. It ran through the heart of our sugar baron's competitor's turf. We wouldn't spare them. Next came the spillway into the North New River Canal. Moving further east we came to the Hillsboro Canal. The last major drainage point was into the Palm Beach Canal. Finally, the Port Mayaca Lock was at the far eastern edge.

We'd take three vehicles with four people each. The two-man teams would approach their target from a distance on foot. The times of arrival would be reported and we'd wait until every man was in place. The gates would open and the water would flow. The fields would be flooded. Either the Corps or our teams would close the gates once the damage was done. We'd all slip away in the dark and regroup back at Fred's house. We had that much figured out. We had not figured out how to manipulate the gates without rendering them inoperable. Hank and a few of his team went to work on that.

I sat down with Brody and Fred to go over the whole plan again. I needed to know if I was missing anything. Was there some detail that we hadn't covered? I normally trusted myself on these things, but after screwing up with the caveman I was a bit less cocky. Fred wanted to find the sea level heights of the two towns in question and that of the cane fields themselves. We had to be certain that we weren't about to kill thousands of innocent people. Brody looked up the information. Clewiston sat up higher than Belle Glade by two feet, but it was dangerously close to the dike. If the dike failed for some reason due to our efforts, there'd be no saving the town or its people. That's why we couldn't just blow the dike and be done with it forever. Big Sugar would survive what we were about to bring down on them, but the idea was to get them off Fred's back. We couldn't sacrifice lives in order to do it.

Hank asked to print out some more photos. They were close-ups of the motors and gears that worked the spillway gates.

"They've got backup generators here behind a chain-link enclosure," he said. "Cutting the power won't work unless we kill the generators too. Might take too long to get power restored."

"Other options?" I asked.

"We blow these motors here and here," he said, pointing at the pictures. "After the gates are open."

"Without the motors, will the gates just fall back into place?" I asked.

"We jam these gears right here," he said. "Stick a piece of rebar or a steel rod between the teeth. If the gates try to go down the rods will lock up the gears."

"The Army Corps just needs to remove the rods and the gates will close," I said. "I like it."

"Even a dogface Army grunt will be able to figure it out pretty quickly," he said.

"They can replace the motors at their leisure," I said. "And use the locks to divert the water flow."

"About that," he said. "I don't think we should jimmy those locks. It will be their last resort if the water can't be held back. It's got to go somewhere. Let's just make sure they stay shut until we're done down at the dike.

It'll take them some time to get access. They'll get to the locks sooner or later and we'll need the gates to work when they do."

"We've got protect those people," said Fred.

"A foot or two of water in their house is bad enough," said Brody. "We can't let the whole damn lake come down on them."

"Okay. We stand by at the locks to keep anyone from opening them, but only until we get the word from Fred that the water needs to stop," I said.

"What if someone shows up?" asks Brody. "Are we going to physically restrain them or what?"

"We'll have to slow them down as best we can," I said. "Make them ask a bunch of questions. Keep the focus on our presence. Point a gun at them if we have to."

"That might work with a civilian lock operator," said Hank. "But it's not a good idea to point a weapon at one of those Army Corps guys. They are still technically soldiers you know."

"Good point," I said. "I'm guessing that they'll call the local operator first. Corps shows up later."

"What do you know about these guys?" he asked.

"I've been through the locks in my boat," I said. "Bunch of old-timers dealing with nervous boaters from seven to five every day."

"We can confront the codgers," he said. "But hands off the Army Corps."

"Agreed," I said.

The plan was coming together. The system of locks and spillways gave us all the tools we needed to move millions of gallons of water out of the lake and onto the cane fields. The monitoring tools allowed us to judge how much damage we'd be doing, and when to stop. We had the gear and the tools appropriate for the job. We only needed the steel rods and a closer look at our targets. We decided to drive the route south of the dike the next day and lay eyeballs on the spillways. That would give us a better feel for how to approach and disable them. We planned to commence with Operation Cane Flood the day after. Fred was deciding what to say when he called his adversary to take credit. Brody and I were looking forward to returning to the mountains. Hank and his men were considering which job offer to accept next. All of us were eager to get this job done.

Eighteen

Our caravan left Fred's house and drove south first thing the next morning. We took Rt. 27 down through Clewiston and on to Belle Glade. From there we picked up Rt. 98 which bordered the lake up to Port Mayaca. On the way back we took a side road towards Pahokee. We stopped at a scenic overlook on Canal Point. The two men assigned to the spillway gates there ambled close in to get the lay of the land. The rest of us pretended to be tourists.

They were reconnoitering for points of entry and an up-close look at the machinery. The control panels were inside a small concrete building with no windows and a locked door. Hank assured me that door locks were no deterrent to entry. Each man carried a tiny concealed camera to photograph the equipment. Once we got what we needed from the first stop, we split up. Two-man teams visited their assigned spillways to do the same recognizance. We all met up back in Clewiston. To help maintain anonymity Hank had sent one of his men up north, over three hundred miles away, to purchase, with construction gloved hands, pre-cut sections of rebar from a Home Depot.

Back at Fred's we all went over the photos. We double checked our maps to identify places to leave the cars that were close enough to get to our targets on foot. We utilized Google Earth to study the terrain between the parking spots and the spillways. Hank's munitions guy produced small C-4 packs that would torch the electric motors. Using the comms system, each team would know when everyone was in place. The little buildings would be breached. The gates would be opened and the steel rod would be jammed in the gears. The teams would take cover nearby and watch for the Army Corps to show up, keeping us all informed. We had no idea how fast they would respond, or if they had enough personnel to close all four spillways at once. If they couldn't get the gates closed before the water got too high, the teams would have to do it themselves. Everyone would then disappear and make their way back to home base. Fred would monitor everything from there.

That night we ate thick steaks and drank cold beer courtesy of Fred. Hank's team was ready. They'd run much more dangerous missions in the Middle East. This would be a walk in the park for them. The only weak link was Brody and me. We weren't Navy SEALs or Special Forces. A suggestion was made to split us up. We could each have one of Hank's men to handle the locks. It was a perfectly reasonable suggestion, but I didn't want to do it. Brody and I were a team. This whole scheme was my idea to begin with. I wanted us to do our part. The Moore Haven Lock was the target closest to Fred's house. We'd be the first ones out if something went wrong. We could handle some seventy-year-old lock operator.

"It's your call," said Hank. "All you'll really be doing is standing guard."

"We'l make sure those gates stay shut until we get the word from Fred," I said. "We'll be fine."

"I've seen Breeze under fire," said Fred. "He keeps his cool. Brody too."

The operation was really quite simple. The disaster that we could cause if it went to hell was what weighed on everyone's mind. We held the fate of thousands of lives in our hands. It was mind-boggling. I needed every team member to understand that.

"I know this mission is probably easier than some of your training exercises," I told the men. "But lives are at stake. Our execution has to be flawless. There can't be any holes in our plan. If any of you have any doubts let's hear them. Tomorrow will be too late."

"I've been thinking about something," said one of Hank's men. "Those metal rods. The gates are heavy. The gears will come down hard on the rods. We might not be able to remove them. We'll need to take the tension off to get the rods out."

"Or the Corps will need to," said Hank. "Without working motors, they'll be stuck open."

"Unless they cut the cables," someone else chimed in.

"We can't be sure they'll be capable of that," I said. "Plus then the gates will be stuck in the closed position. That could compromise the dike."

"What if we leave the motors alone?" asked Brody.

"The Corps shows up and tries to put the gates down," said Hank. "The rods will prevent them. It will take them some time to figure out what's going on, but they will get to it eventually."

"And everything is still in working order when it's all over," I stated.

"What if they get the gates shut before we've flooded the cane fields?" asked Fred. "This will all be for naught."

"That's a possibility," I said. "It will raise some eyebrows at the South Florida Water Management District and the Army Corps of Engineers, but insufficient flooding of crops would be a failure." "What if we force the responders to stand down until we've achieved our objective?" asked Hank.

"That raises the stakes considerably," I said. "What if the cops show up?"

"Okay, bad plan," he said. "Maybe we should go with Brody's idea."

"I think we're going to have to live with the possibility that the fields might not get flooded enough," I said. "We can't risk flooding the towns or damaging the dike. Anyone have any idea how long it will take to get three foot of water on sugar land?"

"The gates vary slightly on the rate of flow," said Fred. "Anywhere from nine thousand cubic feet per second to twelve thousand cubic feet. I'm not an engineer so I don't know how much water that really is. Sounds like a lot. With all the gates open at once, the water should rise rapidly. The canals would overflow within minutes."

"It's a lot of acreage we want to inundate," I said.

Brody looked it up. Ten thousand cubic feet of water equals roughly seventy-five thousand gallons. We'd be releasing that much per gate, per second. That meant four and a half million gallons per minute. In ten minutes we'd let loose forty-five million gallons per gate. It was indeed a lot of water. These calculations led me to believe that it would be up to our team to close the gates before help arrived. There was no way the Corps could respond to every location within ten minutes or even thirty minutes. We decided that we could get the job done without disabling the motors. Raise the gates, wait for Fred's signal, close the gates.

"Do we use the steel rods or not?" I asked.

"If they respond too soon, the rods will slow them down," Hank said. "If the call comes to close the gates before they figure out the rods, we can always just tell them what to do."

"It all boils down to how fast someone shows up to address the problem," I said. "And if it's civilian employees or the Corps."

"That's out of our hands," he said. "Without a dry run, we have no way to know."

"If it happens at three in the morning the response can't be too quick," I said. "I think it's going to work."

Everyone seemed to agree. We packed up all the maps and photos and burned them in the backyard. The C-4 was placed back in the munition guy's car. We all found a place to get some rest. I felt better after we'd aired our doubts and worked out the final details. The worst thing that could happen was the fields wouldn't get flooded enough. The towns would be safe and the equipment would remain intact. I fell asleep feeling positive.

Departure time arrived quickly. Brody and I took two men in Fred's black Range Rover. We dropped them off at the designated spot near the Miami Canal spillway. We back-tracked to the Moore Haven Lock. The other teams advanced on their positions. Our comms were open and working just fine.

Brody and I parked in some trees just down from the entrance road to the lock. We followed the tree line along the road until the facility came into view. We both carried our weapons. The lock itself was dimly lit. With the spillway closed, it was quiet. The water behind the spillway was thick with green algae. I knew that once someone showed up to release the water, that viscous goo would enter the Caloosahatchee River once again, spreading toxins from Moore Haven to Sanibel. It disgusted me, but at least we'd be in the mountains by the time its full effects were felt.

We lay down behind some bushes at the top of a slope. We had a good view of the gate to the spillway. It was locked. We reported into Fred and the other teams that we were on location. An hour passed before all the teams were in place.

"Proceed," said Fred.

In less than fifteen minutes the Miami Canal team reported their gates were open. The three other teams had their gates open within another fifteen minutes. It was happening. We'd started a chain of events that would see a billion or more gallons of water drained from Lake Okeechobee and over the cane fields.

"Water's rising fast," said. Fred. "The canals should be over their banks about now."

We waited in silence. The team at the Hillsborough Canal said that water was backing up at the base of the spillway. The canal wasn't draining off the water fast enough.

"Don't let it eat away at the dike," I said. "Keep an eye on it."

Twenty minutes passed with no response from the SFWMD or the Army Corps.

"I've got one foot of water over the land between the North New River Canal and the Hillsboro Canal," said Fred. "Something's gotta give soon."

The team at the Palm Beach Canal reported responders.

"They look civilian," Hank's man said. "No uniforms. No weapons that I can see."

"We need more time," said Fred.

"They're just getting out of their truck," came the response.

"We've got water encroaching on the berm," said the Hillsborough team. "No response here yet."

"Close a couple gates," I told him. "Slow down the flow."

"Civilian responders at the North New River Canal," came the report.

"All clear at Port Mayaca."

"Still clear at the Miami Canal."

"Clear at Moore Haven," I said.

"Eighteen inches on the gauge," said Fred.

There was radio silence for ten minutes. The suspense was excruciating. Finally, the Hillsborough team reported in.

"We closed two gates," they said. "The berm is dry. Still, a hell of a lot of water flowing."

"Palm Beach here, the responders haven't closed the gates yet. They haven't found the rods."

"Same at New River. They're looking over the equipment with flashlights."

"No response yet at Hillsborough."

"Miami clear."

"Moore Haven clear," I said.

"Mayaca clear."

"Two feet on the gauge," said Fred. "But the rate of rise is slowing. The water is spreading out."

We'd anticipated that. The initial surge would overcome the canal's capacity quickly, but once it rose over the banks and spread out, it would take a lot more water to flood the fifty-thousand acres we were targeting. Once we had three feet of water on the cane fields, it would start approaching the towns. Sirens would sound and all hell would break loose.

That's when we needed to close the gates and escape. Two of the teams already had civilians on site, though the gates remained open.

"Holding steady at two feet," said Fred. "We'll have the Everglades full before we get three feet on those damn cane fields."

"We've got the Army Corps at Hillsborough. We already took the rods out to close those two gates."

"The Palm Beach responders have found the rods. They're trying to knock them out with a hammer. You want me to tell them?"

"Not yet," I said. "We need more water."

"Army Corps at Miami too. Rods still in place."

"Fred?" I said.

"Two foot, three inches," he responded. "The water is almost to Clewiston."

"What about Belle Glade?"

"We've got less water flowing there with those gates closed. Not in danger yet."

"Gates closing at Hillsborough."

"We've got sirens at Palm Beach."

"Hillsborough, get out of there," I said. "Nothing else you can do. Palm Beach run up and show them the rods on your way out."

"North New River here. They've figured it out. Gates closing."

Only the Miami Canal gates remained open, but the Corps was there. It was only a matter of time before they figured out the rods too. Fred reported two feet, six inches. It looked like that was all we could do. It was time to abort the mission.

"Everybody bug out," I said. "Get to your pickup locations. See you back at base."

I heard a car approaching. We crawled a little deeper into the bushes. We watched an older gentlemen get out of the car and walk towards the lock. I didn't want him to open the gates. Our mission was finished and the water level wouldn't make much difference, but I couldn't let the green slime get into the river. I'd hoped all of the water flowing south would carry most of it away. I didn't care if the cane fields got smothered in green goop. I had to stop him.

"Visitor at Moore Haven," I said. "I'm going to see if I can hold him up."

"There's no need, Breeze," said Fred. "Get out of there."

"I'll explain later," I said. "We'll be delayed a bit."

I tried to look non-threatening as I approached the man.

"Evening, sir," I said. "What brings you out here in the middle of the night?"

"I'll ask you the same question," he said. "You're trespassing."

"I was just taking some water samples," I said. "I've got to be to work early."

"You one of them protestors?" he asked. "I'm just doing my job here. That green shit ain't my fault."

"Of course not," I said. "Why's your job got you out here at this hour?"

"Having some trouble down south," he said. "I'm to stand by in case these floodgates gotta be opened."

"In case?"

"Seems they might have things under control," he said. "In which case, these gates can stay shut. Hold back the slime for another day or two."

"Hope it's nothing too serious," I said.

"Might have some wet sugar cane," he said. "Them sugar bosses are probably back pumping into the lake for all their worth."

"Which only makes things worse," I said.

"They're the ones you should be mad at, son," he said. "If you're tossing blame around."

"I don't know why I bother," I said. "Sorry for bothering you too. I've got to run before I'm late for work."

I found Brody and we headed back to the Range Rover.

"On our way to pick up Miami team," I said.

"All the gates are shut," said Fred. "All teams working their way back."

It was over. We didn't know if we'd succeeded or not. We'd have to wait for news to spread. It was a long quiet drive back to Fred's house. Brody and I went straight to bed.

Nineteen

It was all over the news the next morning. Local programs were reporting on the Great Cane Field Flood of 2018. Some speculated that it was the work of eco-terrorists. Some pointed the finger at one of the clean water groups that had been protesting. Field reporters visited the small towns adjacent to the fields. Clewiston had a foot of water in the center of town. They'd seen worse. Belle Glade had half that. It was a nuisance but the property damage was minimal.

Our group was all smiles as we watched a spokesman for Big Sugar being interviewed. He estimated that seventy-five percent of the crop had been lost. He bemoaned the economic impact that it would have on his company. He predicted a sharp increase in sugar prices. He urged law enforcement to find out who was responsible and to prosecute them to the fullest extent of the law.

We hadn't wiped out Big Sugar, but we'd caused them a fair amount of grief. We'd managed to do it without destroying the homes and businesses of Clewiston and Belle Glade. We'd also done it without restarting the harmful discharges into the Caloosahatchee and the St. Lucie Rivers. As a group, we were feeling pretty satisfied with our efforts, but we couldn't claim victory just yet. There was one last order of business.

Fred got a call through to the corporate headquarters of Big Sugar. He got one of the baron brothers on the line.

"Listen to me, you son of a bitch," he said. "That was just a warning. If you don't call off this vendetta against me, it will be ten times worse the next time. Do you understand?"

"I hear you, Mr. Ford," he said.

"Additionally, I'll start a PAC with the express purpose of ending taxpayer subsidies for sugar growers. I'll fund a lobbying effort to stop the restrictions on imported sugar. I will absolutely ruin you. You'll find out how far I will go if you don't get off my back."

"I think we have an understanding," he said.

"So this is over?" asked Fred.

"You'll have no more trouble from us."

Now we could declare success. A cheer went up around the room. Hank and his team had taken a personal interest in the mission and Fred's interests. I thanked each one of them, as did Fred. Before our little party broke up, Fred asked for everyone's attention.

"You guys were great," he said. "I couldn't have asked for a better team. Your efforts are most appreciated and your pay will reflect my thanks. There's a little bonus for each of you on top of what Hank and I agreed upon. Let's not forget my friend Breeze. This was all his idea from the start. The planning was mostly his as well. I can't express my gratitude for this man's contributions to my life. I'm going to miss him and his lovely gal, Brody, but I'm sending them home with a nice bonus as well. Long live Breeze!"

Another round of cheers exploded. The guys patted me on the back and shook my hand again. Brody gave me a hug and a nice long kiss. Her eyes sparkled. All that was left to do was return to our cabin in the mountains. My work in Florida was done.

Twenty

After checking on the cabin, we drove into Banner Elk and had a prime rib dinner at the restaurant we'd visited on our first night in town. Afterwards, I tossed a few logs into the fireplace and we sat in the glow of the flames. We held hands on the couch. I sipped a little rum. We made love in our big new bed and slept the sleep of the victorious.

I snuck out in the morning, letting Brody sleep. I took a thermos of coffee down to my chair at the side of the creek. As I sat down, I caught a flash of color out of the corner of my eye. Could it be?

I donned my polarized sunglasses and studied the running water where I'd seen the flash. I focused in on a washed out piece of the bank that held still water. There he was, a nice fat trout. He was positioned just outside the current, waiting for prey to float by.

It was finally time to buy that fly rod.

Author's Thoughts

My wife and I have decided it's time for a new adventure. By the time you read this, we'll be living in a log cabin in the Blue Ridge Mountains of North Carolina.

Leap of Faith is for sale. You can check her out at this link:

https://www.yachtworld.com/boats/1980/Oceania-36-3226641/Port-Charlotte/FL/United-States#.W0d_x9VKiM8

This will be the **final episode** of the Trawler Trash Series, but don't worry! Our hero will be back in a new series, Mountain Breeze. I'm sure he can find some trouble up in the hill country.

Captain Fred really did build an airport near the cane fields of Florida. The rest of his contributions to this story are pure fiction.

In a previous book in the series, Cool Breeze, I took a stab at addressing the water woes we face in South Florida. It's only gotten worse since then. Red Tide and blue-green algae are real and serious problems. I don't sense a solution anytime soon.

We have thoroughly enjoyed our time aboard a boat in Florida. We've made more memories over the past seven years than most make in a lifetime. It has been my honor to share these stories with my readers. As always, your support is greatly appreciated. Now it's time to move on. Hopefully, I can continue the *Leap of Faith* magic from our new home.

Long Live Breeze!

*If you enjoyed this book, please write a review at Amazon.

Acknowledgements

Proofreaders: Dave Calhoun, Jeanene Olson, Laura Spink

Editor: John Corbin

Cover Photo by Ed Robinson

Cover Design by https://ebooklaunch.com/

Interior Formatting by https://ebooklaunch.com/

Other Books in the Series

Trawler Trash:
https://amzn.to/2E37afw

Following Breeze:
https://amzn.to/2fXJgq2

Free Breeze: https://amzn.to/2fXILfv

Redeeming Breeze:
https://amzn.to/2gbBjAx

Bahama Breeze:
https://amzn.to/2fJiMe6

Cool Breeze: https://amzn.to/2weKg1l

True Breeze:
https://amzn.to/2ws6Hzp

Ominous Breeze:
https://amzn.to/2lPzg70

Restless Breeze:
https://amzn.to/2Aicj0A

Enduring Breeze:
https://amzn.to/2unav5I

Other Books by this Author

Leap of Faith: Quit Your Job and Live on a Boat: https://amzn.to/2L44HbL

Poop, Booze, and Bikinis: https://amzn.to/2LbiwBS

The Untold Story of Kim: https://amzn.to/2ug1Wu7

Made in the USA
Monee, IL
22 September 2020